Contents

An overview of our books for older, catch-up readers

The Alba and Rescue series are two exciting phonic adventure series with strong female as well as male protagonists. They work well with both male and female readers. They have the same phonic pattern and sequence as the Totem and Talisman 1 Series and therefore offer parallel reading experiences. Like the four quest series, they are decodable readers with controlled text and therefore provide fully structured support for students as they learn to read.

The table below shows the over-arching structure of all 6 series for older readers and how they interlink.

All our books for older readers are suitable for readers aged 8 – 14 years.

Series		Who is it aimed at?	What does it cover?
Magic Belt Series (12 reading books and comprehensive workbook)		Students with prior knowledge of the sounds and letters of the alphabet but who need support right from the very beginning of reading	VCC, CVCC, CCVC, CCVCC words and consonant digraphs ch, sh, th, ck, ng, wh, qu and suffixes –ed and –ing
Totem Series (12 reading books and comprehensive workbook)	Parallel text to the Alba series	Students able to read a simple text at CVC level and who know most of the consonant digraphs but have poor knowledge of vowel digraphs	A re-cap of words from CVCC level all the way to CCVCC level and of the consonant digraphs. Introduction of alternative spellings for vowel sounds, e.g. the spellings <ai, ay. ai and a> for the sound 'ae'
Alba Series (12 reading books and comprehensive workbook)	Parallel text to the Totem series	Students able to read a simple text at CVC level and who know most of the consonant digraphs but have poor knowledge of vowel digraphs	A re-cap of words from CVCC level all the way to CCVCC level and of the consonant digraphs. Introduction of alternative spellings for vowel sounds, e.g. the spellings <ai, ay, ai and a> for the sound 'ae'
Talisman 1 Series (10 reading books and comprehensive workbook)	Parallel text to the Rescue series	Students who need support with alternative spellings for vowel sounds	Re-cap of alternative spellings of vowel sounds covered in the Totem series (with additional spellings) progressing to alternative spellings for additional vowel sounds
Rescue Series (10 reading books and comprehensive workbook)	Parallel text to the Talisman 1 series	Students who need support with alternative spellings for vowel sounds	Re-cap of alternative spellings of vowel sounds covered in the Alba series (with additional spellings) progressing to alternative spellings for additional vowel sounds
Talisman 2 Series (10 reading books and comprehensive workbook)		Students who have gaps in their more complex phonic knowledge	More complex spellings for vowel and consonant sounds and suffixes

Notes on the Rescue Series and Workbook

Rescue Series

Introduction
The Rescue Series is aimed at older pupils who need to learn the Phonic Code in order to make progress in their reading. The books introduce the vowel sounds and their alternative spellings. The series includes 10 books, each with a phonic or spelling focus. This workbook, based on the stories, includes a variety of activities which teach and consolidate an understanding of the Phonic Code.

Order of the books
The Rescue Readers can be read out of order, but the storyline works better if they are read in the numbered sequence.

Pronunciation
At the beginning of each book, there is a word list to help the reader learn the alternative spellings of vowel sounds in the English Phonic Code. Pronunciation of some sounds may vary, according to regional accents. The word lists may not always match the pronunciation of the student. This point should be discussed and the lists adapted to the student.

Blending not guessing
Students should be encouraged to blend the sounds into words. If there are spellings they do not know, point to the part of the word that is new and tell them the sound. Then get the student to blend the sounds into the word.

Use precise pronunciation
When blending sounds together, say the consonants without the added 'uh' sound, e.g. 'c' 'a' 't' not 'cuh' 'a' 'tuh'.

Teaching alternative spellings
The English Phonic Code is complex. This series presents up to 7 alternative spellings for a vowel sound. The teacher may need to introduce these spellings gradually if the student has difficulty learning all the alternative spellings at a time.

Splitting multisyllabic words
It is important to teach students how to split multisyllabic words. This will enable them to use successful and independent strategies when reading and spelling long words. There are a number of approaches to splitting multisyllabic words depending on the teaching method:
- A spelling-rules approach, e.g. the doubling rule: s i t / t i ng
- A phonic approach which maintains phoneme/grapheme fidelity, e.g. s i tt / i ng
- A morpheme approach which emphasizes the meaning of parts of the word: l i f t / ed
This workbook allows the teacher to use any method he/she is teaching the student.

New vocabulary
Each new book offers an opportunity to learn new vocabulary on the 'Vocabulary' page. This page explains the words as they appear in the context of the text. The teacher may wish to discuss additional meanings of the word with the student.

The Workbook

This workbook complements the Rescue Series. The 10 chapters in the workbook correlate to the 10 books in the series. Each chapter offers activities based on the phonic focus of each of the books. Before reading the books, students would benefit from practicing word building, blending, reading and sorting activities. These activities feature at the beginning of every chapter. Follow-up activities, such as comprehension, spelling and various games, should be used after reading the texts. The teacher can select from the activities in each chapter to maintain interest and variety.

The chapters for Books 2, 5 and 6 include a sorting activity for a grapheme that represents different sounds. These activities teach the student that he/she may need to try an alternative sound when reading certain graphemes, e.g. <ea> represents different sounds in: br'ea'k, t'ea'm and h'ea'd.

An instruction for every activity in the workbook appears at the bottom of each page.

Phonic sequence in the Rescue Series: Books 1–10

Book	Title	Phoneme focus	Spellings
1	A Great Break	'ae'	ay, ai, a, a-e, ea, ey
2	The Search Begins	'ee'	ee, ea, y, e, ie, e-e, ei
3	Rainbow Fish	'oe'	ow, oa, oe, o-e, o
4	On with the Search	er, ir, ur, or, ear	er, ir, ur, or, ear
5	A Long Way Down	'ow' and 'oi'	ow, ou & oy, oi
6	A Gruesome Monster	'oo'	oo, ue, u-e, ew, ou, u
7	Time is Running Out!	'ie'	igh, ie, i-e, i, y
8	An Awful Planet	aw, awe, a ai, au, ough	aw, awe, a ai, au, ough
9	No Time to Spare	air, are, ear, ere, eir	air, are, ear, ere, eir
10	Dark Times	ar	ar

Rescue Series Activity Book

for Books 1–10

Name: _____

Students can use this page as a personalized front cover for their Rescue Series work.

Book 1: A Great Break
Contents

* 7 things that are not true:
Erin's baby brother is not called Tom; they did not come home by train; Mom was not involved in a project to make things bigger; Erin and Danny did not play on skateboards in the park; Erin was not fetching a sandwich from the kitchen; Jack did not make himself bigger; Erin did not decide to ring her mom to ask for help.

Book 1: Blending and segmenting: 'ae'

rain	r	ai	n	
they				
gate		a	e	
baby				
steak				
train				
plate				
prey				
spray				
snake				
breaking				
making				
fainted				

Blend the sounds into a word. Segment the word into sounds by writing one sound in each square.
Split vowel spellings (a–e) are represented by half squares linked together.
This sheet may be photocopied by the purchaser. © Phonic Books Ltd 2015

Book 1: Reading and sorting words with 'ae' spellings

ai	ay	a	a–e	ea	ey

sale	able	they	faint
great	late	lazy	tray
nail	break	flame	angel
day	pain	steak	mate
David	stay	trail	gray
making	drain	whale	spray
strain	blame	pray	brain
stain	frame	baby	clay

Photocopy this page onto card and cut out the words. Read and sort the cards out
according to the 'ae' headings at the top of the page.
This sheet may be photocopied by the purchaser. © Phonic Books Ltd 2015

Book 1: Reading and spelling words with 'ae' spellings

ai	ay	a–e
_____	_____	_____
_____	_____	_____
_____	_____	_____
_____	_____	_____
_____	_____	_____

a	ea	ey
_____	_____	_____
_____	_____	_____
_____	_____	_____

sale   rain   steak   David   May   late   tray   stain   prey
flame   day   break   whey   chain   spray   blame   great
pain   they   table   fail   fade   baby   clay

List the words according to the 'ae' spellings.

Book 1: Timed reading of words with 'ae' spellings

sale	able	May	faint	shame	late	paint	tray
nail	sacred	flame	quaint	break	they	day	
pain	table	gray	steak	mate	stay	trail	
haze	making	drain	whale	spray	strain		
blame	brain	stain	frame	fade	clay	Spain	

1st try   Time:

---

sale	able	May	faint	shame	late	paint	tray
nail	sacred	flame	quaint	break	they	day	
pain	table	gray	steak	mate	stay	trail	
haze	making	drain	whale	spray	strain		
blame	brain	stain	frame	fade	clay	Spain	

2nd try   Time:

---

sale	able	May	faint	shame	late	paint	tray
nail	sacred	flame	quaint	break	they	day	
pain	table	gray	steak	mate	stay	trail	
haze	making	drain	whale	spray	strain		
blame	brain	stain	frame	fade	clay	Spain	

3rd try   Time:

This timed reading activity is for the student to improve his/her reading speed and fluency. Ask the student to read the words as fast as he/she can. Record the time in the box. Repeat the activity. This sheet can be cut or folded along the dotted lines to allow for different presentations. This sheet may be photocopied by the purchaser. © Phonic Books Ltd 2015

Book 1: Chunking two-syllable words with 'ae'

gatecrash	gate	crash	gatecrash
haystack			
payment			
complain			
breaking			
table			
blameless			
railway			
display			
escape			
steakhouse			
afraid			
awake			
making			

Split the word into two syllables. Write each syllable in a box.
Write the whole word while saying the syllables.

Book 1: Phonic patterns

Color in the words with 'ae' spellings.

understand	trail	great	nailbrush
shame	rubber	flute	black
making	rattle	they	fade
landing	spray	explain	band
dismay	steak	table	delay

Fold this sheet on the dotted line. Read the words in the column on the left. Listen to the sounds in the words. Color in the boxes with words that have 'ae' spellings. Color in the words. Repeat this in the other columns. Unfold the sheet and check the correct words have been colored in.

This sheet may be photocopied by the purchaser. © Phonic Books Ltd 2015

Book 1: Is it true?

Erin lived with her mom and her baby brother, Tom.

They had just had a great break by the beach. They came home by train. When they got home, Mom had to go into the lab. She was involved in a big project making a special ray that helped make things bigger.

Erin's friend, Danny, came to visit and they played on skateboards in the park.

When Danny left, Erin was fetching a sandwich from the kitchen when baby Jack escaped from his bedroom.

Erin found a tiny, red slipper and realized that Jack had made himself bigger!

Erin made a plan to help save baby Jack. She was going to ring her mom at the lab and ask for her help.

There are 7 things in the story above that are not true. Can you spot them?

Ask the student to read the text carefully and circle any false information that has been planted in the story.

Book 1: Picture the scene

Erin is holding the shrink ray in her hand.

A box with an open lid is in front of her.

She is sitting on a rug.

There are milk splashes on the rug.

Behind her is a bookcase.

Book 1: Dictation

Mom had __ __ __ __ __ Erin and __ __ __ __ Jack __ __ ___.

It had been __ __ ___ __ to have a

__ __ ___ __.

When they got back, Mom had to go to her lab to work. Mom had an important job in a lab, working on developing a shrink __ ___. Erin was __ __ __ __ __ __ ___ __ ___ for Jack at home.

Erin's friend, Danny, __ _ __ _ to visit her on his skateboard. ___ ___ _ __ __ __ __ a _ __ _ __ _ _ __ _ on the computer.

Jack found the shrink __ ___! Erin felt __ ___ __ __ with shock. She __ _ __ _ a plan. She was going to use the shrink __ ___ to shrink herself and __ _ __ _ Jack!

Mom had **t a k e n** Erin and **b a b y** Jack **a w ay**. It had been **g r ea t** to have a **b r ea k**.

When they got back, Mom had to go to her lab to work. Mom had an important job in a lab, working on developing a shrink **r ay**. Erin was **b a b y s i tt i ng** for Jack at home.

Erin's friend, Danny, **c a m e** to visit her on his skateboard. **Th ey p l ay ed** a **s p a c e g a m e** on the computer.

Jack found the shrink **r ay**! Erin felt **f ai n t** with shock. She **m a d e** a plan. She was going to use the shrink **r ay** to shrink herself and **s a v e** Jack!

Use the text at the bottom of the page for dictation. The section for dictation can either be cut off by the teacher or folded along the dotted line to allow the student to self-check their spellings on completion. Dictate the passage to the student. Ask her/him to spell the missing words, writing a sound on each line.
Explain that a longer line indicates a spelling with more than one letter, e.g. l igh t.

Book 1: Punctuation activity

Capital letters and full stops

erin was babysitting baby jack she sat in the shade to wait for danny when danny got to her home, he waved from his skateboard he was glad to see erin had a tray of cold milkshakes

There are 8 capital letters and 4 full stops missing.

Did you spot them all?

Book 1: Developing vocabulary: gazed

The word 'gazed' is used here in Book 1:

"Jack is still just a baby," said Erin. "He won't be safe. I must save him. I have to shrink as well." She gazed at the shrink ray. "Mom is going to go crazy..."

'gazed' means: looked at with great interest

Circle the word or phrase that could be replaced with the word 'gazed' in the following text:

The cake smelled of vanilla and was filled with thick red jam. I looked at it longingly as Mom put it on the table.

Can you write two different sentences of your own using the word 'gazed'?

1.

_____

_____

2.

_____

_____

Book 1: Character profile

Use the word bank to help you describe Danny.

playing games   pasta   skateboard   competitions

having fun   sleeping   computer   running

exercise

Name _____

Age _____

Loves _____

Hates *Danny hates having to go to bed!*
_____

Hobbies _____

Favorite food _____

Book 1: Stepping stones reading game 'ae' words

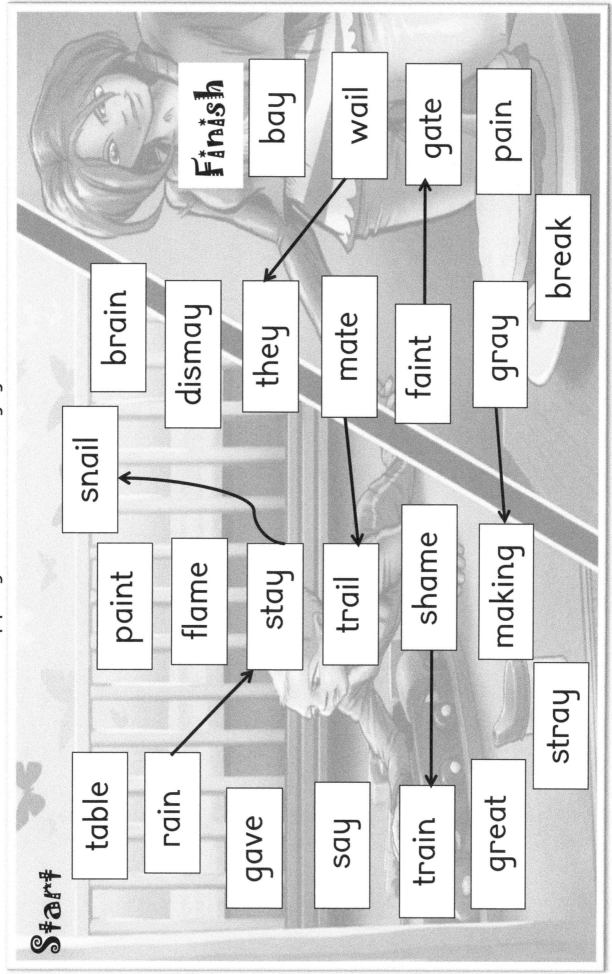

21

A game for 1–4 players: Play with counters and dice.

Players should read aloud the words that they land on at the end of each turn and follow the direction arrows if they land on them.

This sheet may be photocopied by the purchaser. © Phonic Books Ltd 2015

Book 1: Spelling assessment for words with 'ae' spellings

1.

ai	ay	a	a-e	ea	ey
rain	day	baby	name	break	they
faint	play	table	late	steak	prey
brain	spray	bacon	shame	great	whey

2.

ai	ay	a	a-e	ea
sprain	payment	David	gatecrash	breaking
fainted	today	May	blameless	steakhouse
explain	haystack	making		

These lists can be used as a spelling assessment at the end of each book. The teacher can add words from list 2 for students who are ready for that stage. When dictating a word, first say the word on its own. Next, say a sentence with the word in it (to put the word in the context of a sentence) and then repeat the word. This ensures that the student has heard the word correctly, e.g. "Fainted. The boy fainted when he saw the mouse. Fainted."

Book 2: The Search Begins
Contents

* 8 things that are not true:
Erin did not collect things to make a meal of fish and French fries; Erin did not hunt for Jack on the beach next to her home; it was not easy getting to the top of the sink; Erin did not jump from magnet to magnet to reach the top of the sink; Erin did not sit on a plate to cross the sink; Jojo, the rabbit, was not in Erin's way; Erin did not sit on her skateboard to escape from the kitchen; Jojo, the rabbit, did not tug Erin along on her skateboard.

Book 2: Blending and segmenting: 'ee'

feel | f | ee | l

each | ☐ | ☐

theme | ☐ | e | ☐ | e

she | ☐ | ☐

grief | ☐ | ☐ | ☐ | ☐

baby | ☐ | ☐ | ☐ | ☐

delete | ☐ | ☐ | ☐ | ☐ | ☐ | ☐

sheep | ☐ | ☐ | ☐

dream | ☐ | ☐ | ☐ | ☐

shield | ☐ | ☐ | ☐ | ☐

angry | ☐ | ☐ | ☐ | ☐ | ☐

began | ☐ | ☐ | ☐ | ☐ | ☐

scream | ☐ | ☐ | ☐ | ☐ | ☐

Blend the sounds into a word. Segment the word into sounds by writing one sound in each square.
Split vowel spellings (e–e) are represented by half squares linked together.

Book 2: Reading and sorting words with 'ee' spellings

ee	ea	e	ie	ei	e-e	y

reed	seem	she	field
seize	Pete	sunny	messy
creep	sneak	belong	shield
receive	delete	relax	agree
stream	grief	complete	ceiling
indeed	frilly	release	repeat
recede	shriek	begin	scream
feeling	steal	compete	thief

Photocopy this page onto card and cut out the words. Read and sort the cards out
according to the 'ee' headings at the top of the page.
This sheet may be photocopied by the purchaser. © Phonic Books Ltd 2015

Book 2: Reading and spelling words with 'ee' spellings

ee	ea	e
___	___	___
___	___	___
___	___	___
___	___	
___	___	

ie
___
___
___

y	ei	e-e
___	___	___
___	___	___
___	___	___

need   seize   shriek   reach   Pete   me   quickly   green
ceiling   believe   sneak   empty   he   safety   beets   beach
receive   grief   delete   wheel   steam   evil   squeeze
dream   these

List the words according to the 'ee' spellings.

Book 2: Timed reading of words with 'ee' spellings

real   me   keep   chief   leaf   Pete   steam   creep
shield   street   each   delete   steep   easy   belong
seize   relax   deep   happy   field   reef   please
grief   free   messy   theme   treat   sneak   speech
thief   freedom   believe   wheat   cream   funny

1st try   Time:

- -

real   me   keep   chief   leaf   Pete   steam   creep
shield   street   each   delete   steep   easy   belong
seize   relax   deep   happy   field   reef   please
grief   free   messy   theme   treat   sneak   speech
thief   freedom   believe   wheat   cream   funny

2nd try   Time:

- -

real   me   keep   chief   leaf   Pete   steam   creep
shield   street   each   delete   steep   easy   belong
seize   relax   deep   happy   field   reef   please
grief   free   messy   theme   treat   sneak   speech
thief   freedom   believe   wheat   cream   funny

3rd try   Time:

This timed reading activity is for the student to improve his/her reading speed and fluency. Ask the student to read the words as fast as he/she can. Record the time in the box. Repeat the activity. This sheet can be cut or folded along the dotted lines to allow for different presentations.

Book 2: Chunking two-syllable words with 'ee'

freezing	freez	ing	freezing
weaker			
compete			
belief			
creepy			
easy			
evil			
achieve			
ceiling			
agree			
beaten			
complete			
relief			
delete			

Split the word into two syllables. Write each syllable in a box.
Write the whole word while saying the syllables.

Book 2: Phonic patterns

Color in the words with 'ee' spellings.

extreme	beastly	wrench	wished
health	blend	sound	achieve
grieving	bread	ceiling	beaten
gone	stampede	release	dreaming
relax	hungry	evil	Wednesday

Book 2: Is it true?

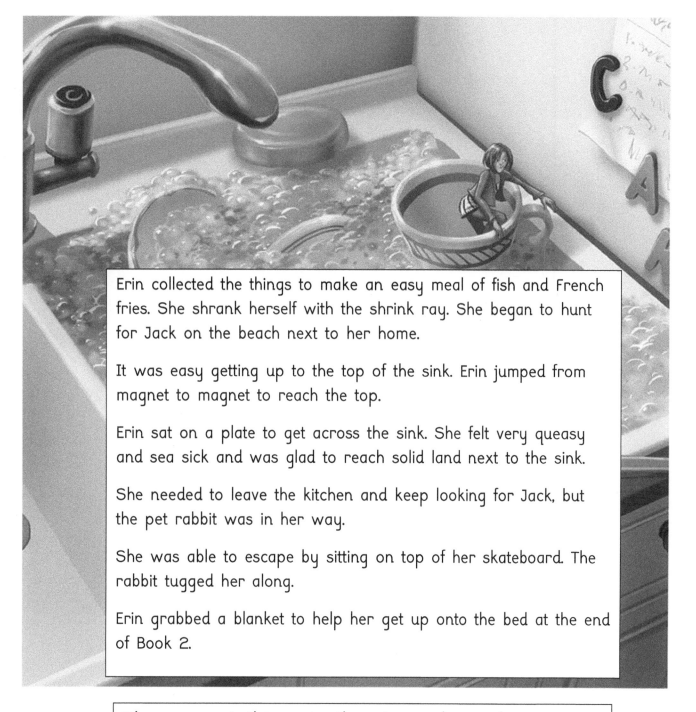

Erin collected the things to make an easy meal of fish and French fries. She shrank herself with the shrink ray. She began to hunt for Jack on the beach next to her home.

It was easy getting up to the top of the sink. Erin jumped from magnet to magnet to reach the top.

Erin sat on a plate to get across the sink. She felt very queasy and sea sick and was glad to reach solid land next to the sink.

She needed to leave the kitchen and keep looking for Jack, but the pet rabbit was in her way.

She was able to escape by sitting on top of her skateboard. The rabbit tugged her along.

Erin grabbed a blanket to help her get up onto the bed at the end of Book 2.

There are 8 things in the story above that are not true. Can you spot them?

Ask the student to read the text carefully and circle any false information that has been planted in the story.
This sheet may be photocopied by the purchaser. © Phonic Books Ltd 2015

Book 2: Picture the scene

Erin is jumping off a fridge magnet shaped like a capital letter 'A'.

She is landing on a rug.

In front of her is a massive wheel.

She has soapy bubbles on her feet from the sink.

A candy as big as a beach ball is on the corner of the rug.

Book 2: Dictation

It was a long way to the top and Erin felt __ ___ __ at the

kn ___ __.

" __ __ __ __ __ and __ ___ __   __ __ ___ ___ __ ___,"

she told herself. "I'll __ __ __ __ __ __ __ this is a __ __ ___

on the __ ___ ___."

In her __ ___ __ __ ___ __, waves lapped __ __ __ __ __ __

on the sand.

Erin __ ___ __ ___ the rim of a __ ___ cup and sailed

across the sink.

Erin __ __ __ __ __ to __ ___ __   __ ___ __ __ ___.

It was a __ __ __ ___ __ to __ ___ ___ solid land next to

the sink.

It was a long way to the top and Erin felt **w ea k** at the **kn ee s**.

"**R e l a x** and **k ee p   b r ea th i ng**," she told herself. "I'll **p r e t e n d** this is a **t r ee** on the

b ea ch."

In her **d ay d r ea m,** waves lapped **g e n t l y** on the sand.

Erin **s ei z ed** the rim of a **t ea** cup and sailed across the sink.

Erin **b e g a n** to **f ee l s ea s i ck**.

It was a **r e l ie f** to **r ea ch** solid land next to the sink.

Use the text at the bottom of the page for dictation. The section for dictation can either be cut off by the teacher or folded along the dotted line to allow the student to self-check their spellings on completion. Dictate the passage to the student. Ask her/him to spell the missing words, writing a sound on each line.
Explain that a longer line indicates a spelling with more than one letter, e.g. l igh t.

Book 2: Punctuation activity

Capital letters and full stops

the lapping waves were really in the sink pots and pans bobbed in streams of bubbles erin seized the rim of a tea cup and jumped in she paddled across the sink it was a relief to see solid land

There are 5 capital letters and 5 full stops missing.

Did you spot them all?

Ask the student to read through the text and add in capital letters and full stops where necessary. Encourage the student to read aloud as this will help him/her identify where the sentences stop.
This sheet may be photocopied by the purchaser. © Phonic Books Ltd 2015

Book 2: Developing vocabulary: weaving

The word 'weaving' is used here in Book 2:

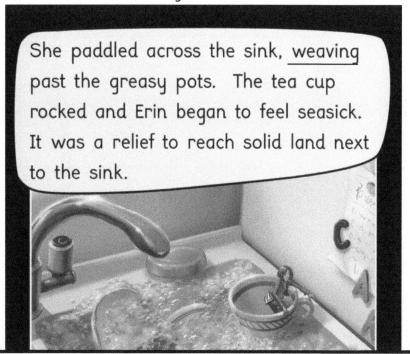

She paddled across the sink, weaving past the greasy pots. The tea cup rocked and Erin began to feel seasick. It was a relief to reach solid land next to the sink.

'weaving' means: moving from side to side to avoid things that are in the way.

Circle the word or phrase that could be replaced with the word 'weaving' in the following piece of text:

My best pal and I were chasing each other in the street. It had been raining for days and the street was full of deep puddles. I hated getting wet feet! As I ran away from him, I was running from side to side past the puddles.

Can you write two different sentences of your own using the word 'weaving'?

1.

_____

_____

2.

_____

_____

Book 2: Character profile

Use the word bank to help you describe Ziggy, the cat.

playing games

pasta

hunting

chasing

having fun

sleeping

eating

exercise

being cuddled

Name _____

Age _____

Loves *Ziggy loves stealing hot fish from the dinner table!*
_____

_____

Hates _____

Hobbies _____

Favorite food _____

This is a writing frame to help structure creative writing. Ask the student to use words from the word bank to help them create a character profile for Ziggy, the cat. They will know some things from the story, but encourage them to be creative in their answers and to try to write in full sentences, using capital letters and full stops. This framework can also be used as a planning document for a piece of free writing.

Book 2: Stepping stones reading game 'ee' words

37

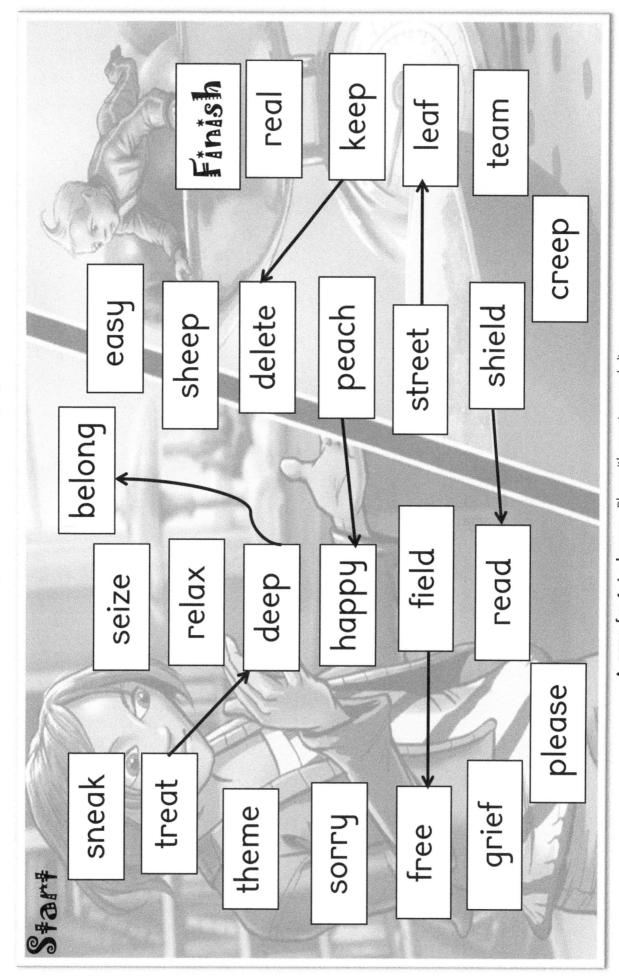

Start

Finish

sneak treat theme sorry free grief please

seize relax deep happy field read

belong

easy sheep delete peach street shield creep

real keep leaf team

Book 2: Spelling assessment for words with 'ee' spellings

1.

ee	ea	e	e–e	y	ei	ie
feet	sea	me	Pete	funny	ceiling	chief
sheep	meat	she	theme	happy		thief
breed	bleak	relax	delete	floppy		shield

2.

ee	ea	e	e–e	y	ei	ie
greed	dream	evil	compete	badly	seize	priest
agree	bleach	begin	complete	angry	receive	piece
screech	scream	belong	athlete	hungry		shriek

These lists can be used as a spelling assessment at the end of each book. The teacher can add words from list 2 for students who are ready for that stage. When dictating a word, first say the word on its own. Next, say a sentence with the word in it (to put the word in the context of a sentence) and then repeat the word. This ensures that the student has heard the word correctly, e.g. "Fainted. The boy fainted when he saw the mouse. Fainted."

Book 3: Rainbow Fish
Contents

* 7 things that are not true:
Erin did not spot something pink in the fish tank; Erin did not grab a pen to take in the tank with her; Erin was not nudged by a black, spotted fish; the flag on top of the model boat was not yellow; the boat was not full of holes; the boat did not sink; Erin did not hug the dolls.

Book 3: Blending and segmenting: 'oe'

row | r | ow |

go

hope | | o | | e |

toe

most

roast

slope

foe

groan

stone

snowing

floats

joking

Blend the sounds into a word. Segment the word into sounds by writing one sound in each square.
Split vowel spellings (o–e) are represented by half squares linked together.
This sheet may be photocopied by the purchaser. © Phonic Books Ltd 2015

Book 3: Reading and sorting words with 'oe' spellings

o	oa	ow	o-e	oe

toe	bold	bone	coat
rope	go	hole	bow
joke	most	pole	show
groan	hold	float	goes
snow	spoke	shoal	broken
roast	flow	goat	note
alone	toast	crow	close
know	soap	Rome	hero

Book 3: Reading and spelling words with 'oe' spellings

ow	oa	o–e
_____	_____	_____
_____	_____	_____
_____	_____	_____
_____	_____	_____
_____	_____	_____

o	oe
_____	_____
_____	_____
_____	_____

so   snow   woe   roast   hope   road   blow   groan
show   joke   no   throat   foe   grow   bone   bloat   go
drove   toe   throw   spoke

List the words according to the 'oe' spellings.

Book 3: Timed reading of words with 'oe' spellings

so   snow   woe   roast   hope   road   blow
groan   show   no   throw   foe   grow   bone
bloat   go   drove   toe   flow   spoke   pole   loan
low   know   roll   hole   cope   most   coat   mole
crow   moan   slope   goat   toad

1st try	Time:

---

so   snow   woe   roast   hope   road   blow
groan   show   no   throw   foe   grow   bone
bloat   go   drove   toe   flow   spoke   pole   loan
low   know   roll   hole   cope   most   coat   mole
crow   moan   slope   goat   toad

2nd try	Time:

---

so   snow   woe   roast   hope   road   blow
groan   show   no   throw   foe   grow   bone
bloat   go   drove   toe   flow   spoke   pole   loan
low   know   roll   hole   cope   most   coat   mole
crow   moan   slope   goat   toad

3rd try	Time:

This timed reading activity is for the student to improve his/her reading speed and fluency. Ask the student to read the words as fast as he/she can. Record the time in the box. Repeat the activity. This sheet can be cut or folded along the dotted lines to allow for different presentations.

Book 3: Chunking two-syllable words with 'oe'

open	o	pen	open
hopeless			
moaning			
narrow			
woeful			
joking			
lonely			
boastful			
tiptoe			
borrow			
hero			
homeless			
oboe			
widow			

Split the word into two syllables. Write each syllable in a box.
Write the whole word while saying the syllables.
This sheet may be photocopied by the purchaser. © Phonic Books Ltd 2015

Book 3: Phonic patterns

Color in the words with 'oe' spellings.

cotton	boast	broken	spotted
shopping	crow	belong	float
joking	got	cope	snowman
follow	aunt	pillow	spoke
rope	below	throat	job

Book 3: Is it true?

Erin spots something pink floating in a fish tank. She thinks Jack may be in the tank! She grabs a pen from next to her and dives into the tank with it.

A black, spotted fish nudges Erin's elbow and tickles her. Erin probes between the rocks to see if she can find Jack. A massive fish floats over her and Erin gets into a plastic barrel to get away from it.

Erin spots a model boat at the bottom of the tank. The flag on the boat was the yellow cloth she had seen! Jack was not in the tank.

Erin drags the boat up to the top of the tank, but it is full of holes and sinks to the bottom!

Erin clambers up a hose hanging over the tank. She hugs the dolls next to the tank.

There are 7 things in the story above that are not true. Can you spot them?

Ask the student to read the text carefully and circle any false information that has been planted in the story.

Book 3: Picture the scene

Erin is swimming under a boat.

She is holding a rope that is connected to the boat.

The boat has a flag on it.

Six fish are floating in the tank next to Erin.

There are five rocks underneath her.

Book 3: Dictation

Erin had seen a flash of red cloth __ __ ___ __ __ ___ in the fish tank.

She held her __ __ __ __ and jumped into the bubbling __ ___ __ that was __ __ ___ __ __ ___ in the tank.

A ___ ___ __ of __ ___ __ __ ___ fish __ __ ___ __ ___ next to Erin and tickled her __ ___ __!

The ___ __ __ ___ of a big fish fell over her. Erin hid inside a plastic jellyfish. She kept as still as a __ __ __ __ __. The fish nudged her __ __ __ ___!

Erin reached a model __ ___ __. She dragged it up to the top of the tank and __ ___ ___ it across to a __ __ __ __.

She clambered up the __ __ __ __ to get out of the tank.

Erin had seen a flash of red cloth **f l oa t i ng** in the fish tank.

She held her **n o s e** and jumped into the bubbling **f oa m** that was **f l oa t i ng** in the tank.

A **sh oa l** of **r ai n b ow** fish **f l oa t ed** next to Erin and tickled her **t oe s**!

The **sh a d ow** of a big fish fell over her. Erin hid inside a plastic jellyfish. She kept as still as a **s t o n e**. The fish nudged her **e l b ow**.

Erin reached a model **b oa t**. She dragged it up to the top of the tank and **r ow ed** it across to a **h o s e**. She clambered up the **h o s e** to get out of the tank.

Book 3: Punctuation activity

Capital letters, full stops and question marks

erin had seen a flash of red cloth
floating in the fish tank was it jack's
sock she jumped onto the shelf and
gazed into the tank she grabbed an old
stick that was at the end of the shelf
and jumped into the bubbling foam

There are 5 capital letters, 3 full stops and 1 question mark
missing.

Did you spot them all?

Ask the student to read through the text and add in capital letters, full stops and question marks
where necessary. Encourage the student to read aloud as this will help him/her identify where the
sentences stop.

Book 3: Developing vocabulary: nudged

The word 'nudged' is used here in Book 3:

A shoal of rainbow fish floated so close to Erin that they tickled her. Red and yellow fish followed her and <u>nudged</u> her toes. "Get off!" giggled Erin as the fish swam off.

'nudged' means: pushed slightly or gently

Circle the word or phrase that could be replaced with the word 'nudged' in the following text:

The tea cup was very close to the edge of the sofa. As she sat down, her handbag bumped it softly. Hot tea ran in a sudden hot stream across the seat.

Can you write two different sentences of your own using the word 'nudged'?

1.

_____

_____

2.

_____

_____

Book 3: Character profile

Use the word bank to help you describe Erin.

hopeful   practical jokes   swimming   kind

having fun   brave   sleeping   afraid of heights

keeping fit   computer games

Name _____

Age _____

Loves _____

Hates _____

Hobbies _____

Favorite food _____

Erin loves hot toast with jam and roast chicken!

This is a writing frame to help structure creative writing. Ask the student to use words from the word bank to help them create a character profile for Erin. They will know some things from the story, but encourage them to be creative in their answers and to try to write in full sentences, using capital letters and full stops. This framework can also be used as a planning document for a piece of free writing.

Book 3: Stepping stones reading game 'oe' words

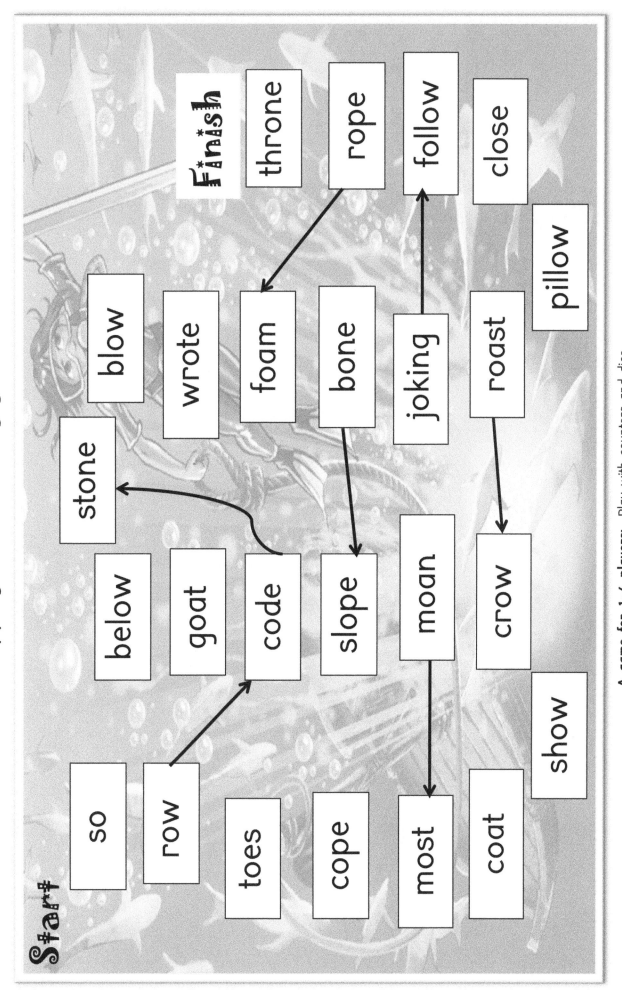

53

Book 3: Spelling assessment for words with 'oe' spellings

1.

oa	ow	o-e	o	oe
toad	low	hope	go	toe
coast	show	choke	no	hoe
broach	flown	stroke	hero	woe

2.

oa	ow	o-e	o	oe
boastful	window	lonely	joking	tiptoe
floating	shadow	hopeful	broken	woeful
groaned	slowly			

These lists can be used as a spelling assessment at the end of each book. The teacher can add words from list 2 for students who are ready for that stage. When dictating a word, first say the word on its own. Next, say a sentence with the word in it (to put the word in the context of a sentence) and then repeat the word. This ensures that the student has heard the word correctly, e.g. "Fainted. The boy fainted when he saw the mouse. Fainted."

Book 4: On with the Search
Contents

* 7 things that are not true:
Erin was not scared that Jack was in the hamster's cage; Jojo was not munching on an apple; Erin did not help Jojo chew his way out of the cage; Erin did not make a saddle from a plastic bag; Jack was not in the bath; Erin did not use a rubber ring to rescue Jack; Jack had not ridden upstairs on the back of a beetle.

Book 4: Blending and segmenting: er, ir, ur, or, ear spellings

fur	f	ur		
sir				
term				
word				
earn				
church				
twirl				
nerve				
worth				
learn				
burst				
skirt				
world				

Blend the sounds into a word. Segment the word into sounds by writing one sound in each square.

Book 4: Reading and sorting words with er, ir, ur, or, ear spellings

er	ur	ir	or	ear

world	earn	purse	jerk
her	first	burp	worm
early	bird	serve	turn
worth	heard	curl	curb
dirty	verse	work	learn
curse	worse	birth	whirl
murder	sister	stir	expert
search	worship	disturb	further

Book 4: Reading and spelling words with er, ir, ur, or, ear spellings

er
_____
_____
_____
_____
_____

ur
_____
_____
_____
_____
_____

ir
_____
_____
_____
_____
_____

or
_____
_____
_____

ear
_____
_____
_____

her	first	burp	worm	world	earn	purse	bird

her first burp worm world earn purse bird
serve turn birth heard dirty work sister verb
earth burnt fur girl verse

List the words according to their spellings.

Book 4: Timed reading of words with er, ir, ur, or, ear spellings

her	fir	earn	word	hurt	shirt	yearn	work
turn	fern	learn	world	burp	sister	further	
early	dirty	worth	firm	church	search	enter	
worm	term	skirt	germ	heard	father	over	
firm	burnt	verse	worse				

1st try   Time:

- -

her	fir	earn	word	hurt	shirt	yearn	work
turn	fern	learn	world	burp	sister	further	
early	dirty	worth	firm	church	search	enter	
worm	term	skirt	germ	heard	father	over	
firm	burnt	verse	worse				

2nd try   Time:

- -

her	fir	earn	word	hurt	shirt	yearn	work
turn	fern	learn	world	burp	sister	further	
early	dirty	worth	firm	church	search	enter	
worm	term	skirt	germ	heard	father	over	
firm	burnt	verse	worse				

3rd try   Time:

This timed reading activity is for the student to improve his/her reading speed and fluency. Ask the student to read the words as fast as he/she can. Record the time in the box. Repeat the activity. This sheet can be cut or folded along the dotted lines to allow for different presentations.

Book 4: Chunking two-syllable words with er, ir, ur, or, ear spellings

word	syll 1	syll 2	whole
person	per	son	person
thirteen			
murder			
earning			
worship			
thirsty			
disturb			
expert			
early			
worker			
birthday			
further			
permit			
worthless			

Split the word into two syllables. Write each syllable in a box.
Write the whole word while saying the syllables.

Book 4: Phonic patterns

Color in the words with er, ir, ur, or and ear spellings.

sister	worth	bunting	circle
further	early	butter	drastic
head	purple	church	nurse
heard	word	first	birthday
instead	wobble	blister	murmur

Fold this sheet on the dotted line. Read the words in the column on the left. Listen to the sounds in the words. Color in the boxes with words that have er, ir, ur, or, or ear spellings. Repeat this in the other columns. Unfold the sheet and check the correct words have been colored in.

This sheet may be photocopied by the purchaser. © Phonic Books Ltd 2015

Book 4: Is it true?

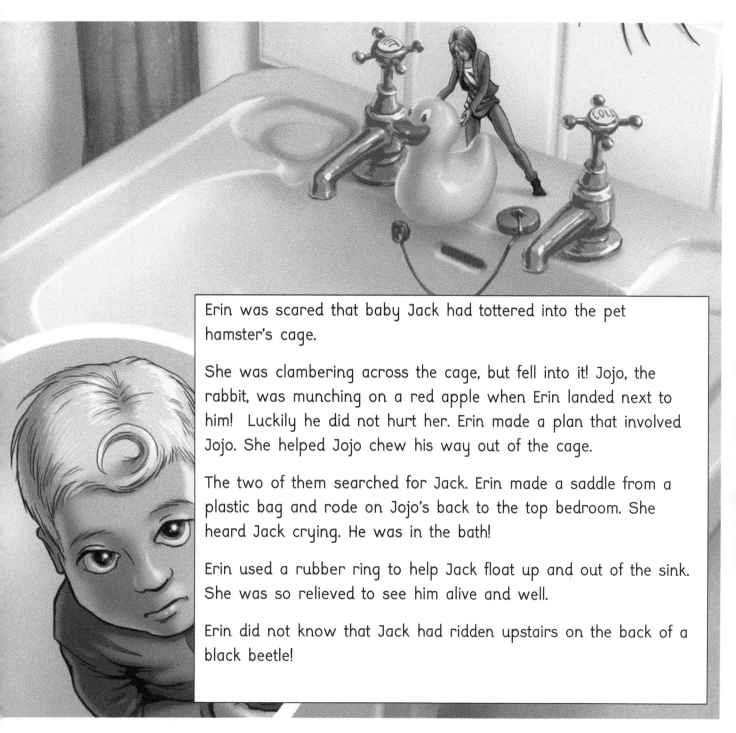

Erin was scared that baby Jack had tottered into the pet hamster's cage.

She was clambering across the cage, but fell into it! Jojo, the rabbit, was munching on a red apple when Erin landed next to him! Luckily he did not hurt her. Erin made a plan that involved Jojo. She helped Jojo chew his way out of the cage.

The two of them searched for Jack. Erin made a saddle from a plastic bag and rode on Jojo's back to the top bedroom. She heard Jack crying. He was in the bath!

Erin used a rubber ring to help Jack float up and out of the sink. She was so relieved to see him alive and well.

Erin did not know that Jack had ridden upstairs on the back of a black beetle!

There are 7 things in the story above that are not true. Can you spot them?

Ask the student to read the text carefully and circle any false information that has been planted in the story.

Book 4: Picture the scene

Jojo, the rabbit, is eating a long carrot.

He has three chunks of red pepper next to him.

Erin is dropping into the cage and landing on top of him!

There is lots of hay underneath Jojo.

There is a flower in the straw.

Book 4: Dictation

Erin had __ ____ ____ ____ most of her home.

She __ __ __ __ __ ____ ____ across Jojo's cage to see if Jack was inside.

She fell into the cage and landed next to Jojo! She patted his soft __ ____ with her __ __ __ __ ____ __.

Jojo was amazed to see a __ ____ __ as big as a carrot! He did not __ ____ __ Erin. He let __ ____ __ __ __ __ __ ____ up onto his back and they went up to the attic.

Erin __ ____ __ baby Jack crying! He was in the sink.

Erin helped Jack float up to the top of the sink on the __ __ ____ ____ duck.

Erin was so glad to see him alive and well. She did not know he had ridden to the attic on the back of a __ __ __ __ ____!

Erin had **s** **ear** **ch** **ed** most of her home. She **c** **l** **a** **m** **b** **er** **ed** across Jojo's cage to see if Jack was inside.

She fell into the cage and landed next to Jojo! She patted his soft **f** **ur** with her **f** **i** **n** **g** **er** **s**.

Jojo was amazed to see a **g** **ir** **l** as big as a carrot! He did not **h** **ur** **t** Erin. He let **h** **er** **c** **l** **am** **b** **er** up onto his back and they went up to the attic.

Erin **h** **ear** **d** baby Jack crying! He was in the sink.

Erin helped Jack float up to the top of the sink on the **r** **u** **bb** **er** duck.

Erin was so glad to see him alive and well. She did not know he had ridden to the attic on the back of a **s** **p** **i** **d** **er**!

Book 4: Punctuation activity

Capital letters, full stops and question marks

jojo was sitting, munching on a crispy carrot he was a great pet he was easy to feed and happy to be cuddled he had never bitten erin or jack had jack tottered into jojo's hutch

There are 9 capital letters, 4 full stops and 1 question mark missing.

Did you spot them all?

Ask the student to read through the text and add in capital letters, full stops and question marks where necessary. Encourage the student to read aloud as this will help him/her identify where the sentences stop.

Book 4: Developing vocabulary: clamber

The word 'clamber' is used here in Book 4:

> The silver pin dropped with a clatter and Jojo raced along the hall. The eager rabbit began to <u>clamber</u> up the steep steps that led to the attic.

'clamber' means: to climb with effort or difficulty, using both hands and feet

Circle the word or phrase that could be replaced with the word 'clamber' in the following text:

The boat was swaying crazily in the strong wind. Jez held his breath. Using both hands and feet, he began to climb up the rope hanging from the sail.

Can you write two different sentences of your own using the word 'clamber'?

1.

_____

_____

2.

_____

_____

Book 4: Character profile

Use the word bank to help you describe Jojo, the rabbit.

playing with Jack   escaping

crunchy   vegetables

having fun

exercise   sleeping   drinking water

Name _____

Age _____

Loves _Jojo loves being cuddled and hugged!_
_____

Hates _____

Hobbies _____

Favorite food _____

This is a writing frame to help structure creative writing. Ask the student to use words from the word bank to help them create a character profile for Jojo. They will know some things from the story, but encourage them to be creative in their answers and to try to write in full sentences, using capital letters and full stops. This framework can also be used as a planning document for a piece of free writing.

Book 4: Stepping stones reading game: er, ir, ur, or, ear

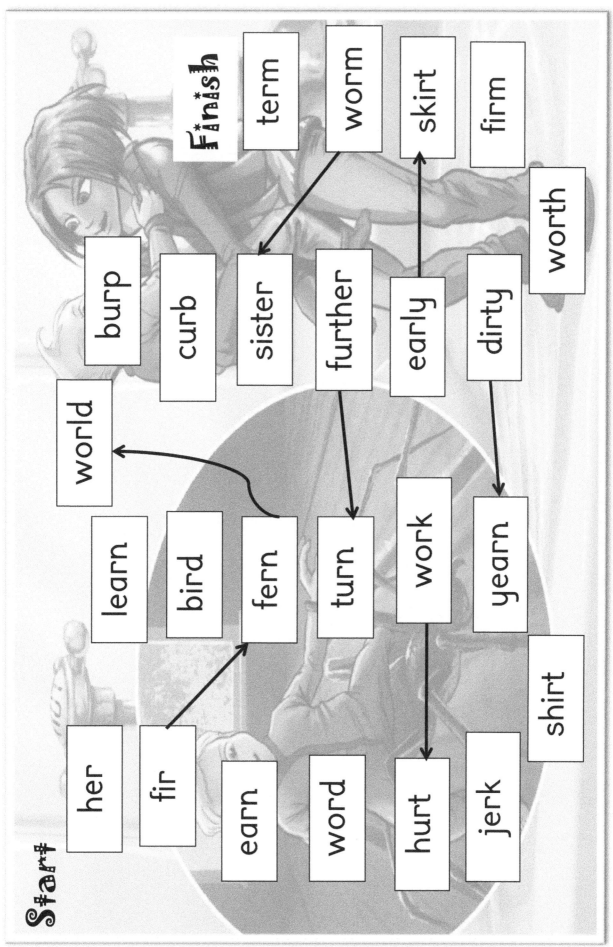

Start

her	world	burp	Finish
fir	learn	curb	term
earn	bird	sister	worm
word	fern	further	skirt
work	turn	early	firm
hurt	yearn	dirty	worth
jerk	shirt		

A game for 1–4 players: Play with counters and dice.
Players should read aloud the words that they land on at the end of each turn and follow the direction arrows if they land on them.
This sheet may be photocopied by the purchaser. © Phonic Books Ltd 2015

Book 4: Spelling assessment for words with er, ir, ur, or, ear spellings

1.

er	ir	ur	ear	or
her	sir	hurt	pearl	word
serve	bird	curl	search	work
nerve	first	turn	heard	worm

2.

er	ir	ur	ear	or
over	stir	burnt	early	world
finger	twirl	church	earned	worth
hunger	birthday	disturb	earnest	worse

Book 5: A Long Way Down
Contents

* 6 things that are not true:
Erin did not pretend to be a clown; Jack did not hold on to Erin's leg; Jojo, the rabbit, did not jump out at Erin and Jack; Erin did not make an antidote with milk and a crushed leaf; Jack and Erin did not sit in the pod eating chunks of apple; Erin and Jack were not transported into the garden.

Book 5: Blending and segmenting: 'ow'

out	ou	t			
how					
loud					
town					
pouch					
brown					
sound					
drown					
mouth					
scowl					
ground					
howling					
about					

Blend the sounds into a word. Segment the word into sounds by writing one sound in each square.

Book 5: Blending and segmenting: 'oi'

oil	oi	l			
toy					
boy					
coin					
soya					
voice					
enjoy					
spoil					
loyal					
avoid					
annoy					
toilet					
employ					

Blend the sounds into a word. Segment the word into sounds by writing one sound in each square.
This sheet may be photocopied by the purchaser. © Phonic Books Ltd 2015

Book 5: Reading and sorting words
with 'ow' and 'oi' spellings

ow		**ou**	
howl	round	aloud	tower
ouch	power	shout	frown
allow	spout	shower	bound

oi		**oy**	
boy	enjoy	point	toilet
soil	toy	royal	voice
annoy	coin	destroy	spoilt

Book 5: Reading and spelling words with 'ow' and 'oi' spellings

ow	ou
_____	_____
_____	_____
_____	_____
_____	_____
_____	_____

shout   how   power   mound   sound   scout   clown
brown   drown   house   gown   found

oi	oy
_____	_____
_____	_____
_____	_____
_____	_____

toy   spoil   enjoy   point   ploy   foil
avoid   boy   employ

List the words according to the 'ow' and 'oi' spellings.

Book 5: Timed reading of words with 'ow' spellings

fowl   loud   round   town   pout   house   mount
allow   proud   howl   crowd   how   sound   noun
vowel   spout   frown   brow   towel   growl
found   hound   brown   wow   cloud   clown
ground   mouse   scout   discount   trowel

1st try	**Time:**

- -

fowl   loud   round   town   pout   house   mount
allow   proud   howl   crowd   how   sound   noun
vowel   spout   frown   brow   towel   growl
found   hound   brown   wow   cloud   clown
ground   mouse   scout   discount   trowel

2nd try	**Time:**

- -

fowl   loud   round   town   pout   house   mount
allow   proud   howl   crowd   how   sound   noun
vowel   spout   frown   brow   towel   growl
found   hound   brown   wow   cloud   clown
ground   mouse   scout   discount   trowel

3rd try	**Time:**

Book 5: Timed reading of words with 'oi' spellings

toil	boy	noise	toy	spoil	soya	boil
voice	joy	coin	poise	annoy	coil	point
oil	joint	toilet	royal	oyster	employ	
enjoy	foil	loyal	poison	avoid	ointment	
	decoy	destroy	soil	boiling		

1st try   Time:

- -

toil	boy	noise	toy	spoil	soya	boil
voice	joy	coin	poise	annoy	coil	point
oil	joint	toilet	royal	oyster	employ	
enjoy	foil	loyal	poison	avoid	ointment	
	decoy	destroy	soil	boiling		

2nd try   Time:

- -

toil	boy	noise	toy	spoil	soya	boil
voice	joy	coin	poise	annoy	coil	point
oil	joint	toilet	royal	oyster	employ	
enjoy	foil	loyal	poison	avoid	ointment	
	decoy	destroy	soil	boiling		

3rd try   Time:

Book 5: Chunking two-syllable words with 'ow'

loudest	loud	est	loudest
power			
pouting			
drowsy			
voucher			
outing			
grounded			
towel			
bouncy			
howling			
mouthful			
flower			
rebound			
crowded			

Split the word into two syllables. Write each syllable in a box.
Write the whole word while saying the syllables.
This sheet may be photocopied by the purchaser. © Phonic Books Ltd 2015

Book 5: Chunking two-syllable words with 'oi'

employ	*em*	*ploy*	*employ*
oily			
convoy			
poison			
toilet			
destroy			
avoid			
decoy			
noisy			
annoy			
boiling			
royal			
ointment			
enjoy			

Split the word into two syllables. Write each syllable in a box.
Write the whole word while saying the syllables.
This sheet may be photocopied by the purchaser. © Phonic Books Ltd 2015

Book 5: Reading and sorting words with <ow> spelling

snow	cow

howl	growl	mow	bow
now	blow	low	tow
flow	know	crown	crow
allow	glow	brow	town
slow	show	brown	fowl
jowl	power	bowl	row
vow	throw	trowel	towel
down	shower	yellow	flower

Book 5: Phonic patterns

Color in only words with the spelling <ow> that is pronounced 'ow' as in 'clown'.

blow	down	throw	crown
frown	crowd	crow	howl
show	mellow	shower	tower
drown	flower	owl	know
how	town	flow	low

Fold this sheet on the dotted line. Read the words in the column on the left. Listen to the sounds in the words. Color in the boxes with words that have the spelling <ow> that is pronounced 'ow'. Repeat this in the other columns. Unfold the sheet and check the correct words have been colored in.

This sheet may be photocopied by the purchaser. © Phonic Books Ltd 2015

Book 5: Is it true?

Baby Jack was sad and hungry. Erin played a game to make him happy. She pretended to be a clown.

Erin clambered down to the ground with Jack holding on to her leg. She was about to feed Jack the shrinking antidote when Jojo, the rabbit, jumped out at them.

They got away, but the antidote had all been spilled. They hid in a closet.

Erin was able to make another bottle of antidote using a crushed leaf and a cup of milk.

Erin remembered Mom's electric shrink reversal pod. She and Jack sat in the pod eating chunks of apple.

When Erin plugged a cable into the pod, she and Jack were transported into the garden!

There are 6 things in the story above that are not true. Can you spot them?

Book 5: Picture the scene

Erin is sitting on a toothbrush.

Baby Jack is in front of her.

A big rubber duck is behind her.

There is a big spider on the wall.

The spider has spun a web next to him.

Book 5: Dictation

Erin galloped __ __ ___ __ __ Jack on a toothbrush, making

__ ___ __ __ __ like a donkey. She told jokes in a funny

__ ___ ___. Jack giggled and stopped __ __ ___ __ __ ___.
He was such a brave __ ___.

They clambered __ ___ __ to the __ __ ___ __ __ by gripping
onto a __ ___ ___.

They __ ___ __ __ the picnic and ate a __ ___ __ __ of apple
chunks. Ziggy, the cat, was just about to __ ___ __ ___ on
them!

They ran away, but the antidote was spilled.

Erin and Jack got into the electric pod Mom had made to reverse
the shrinking. When Erin plugged in a cable, the pod twirled

__ ___ __ __ and __ __ ___ __ __. It made lots of __ ___ ___.

Erin and Jack had been transported into the space game!

Erin galloped **a r ou n d** Jack on a toothbrush, making **s ou n d s** like a donkey. She told jokes in a funny **v oi ce**. Jack giggled and stopped **f r ow n i ng**. He was such a brave **b oy**.

They clambered **d ow n** to the **g r ou n d** by gripping onto a **t ow el**. They **f ou n d** the picnic and ate a **m ou n d** of apple chunks. Ziggy, the cat, was just about to **p ou n ce** on them! They ran away, but the antidote was spilled.

Erin and Jack got into the electric pod Mom had made to reverse the shrinking. When Erin plugged in a cable, the pod twirled **r ou n d** and **a r ou n d**. It made lots of **n oi se**. Erin and Jack had been transported into the space game!

Use the text at the bottom of the page for dictation. The section for dictation can either be cut off by the teacher or folded along the dotted line to allow the student to self-check their spellings on completion. Dictate the passage to the student. Ask her/him to spell the missing words, writing a sound on each line.
Explain that a longer line indicates a spelling with more than one letter, e.g. l igh t.
This sheet may be photocopied by the purchaser. © Phonic Books Ltd 2015

Book 5: Punctuation activity

Capital letters, full stops and speech marks

Remember you will still need to use capital letters <u>inside</u> your speech marks.

jack sat down with a bump his mouth turned down and his bottom lip began to quiver stay strong, baby boy, whispered erin as she hugged him when she galloped around jack on a toothbrush making sounds like a donkey, it made him giggle

There are 6 capital letters, 4 full stops and 1 set of speech marks missing.

Did you spot them all?

Ask the student to read through the text and add in capital letters, full stops and speech marks where necessary. Encourage the student to read aloud as this will help him/her identify where the sentences stop.

Book 5: Developing vocabulary: quiver

The word 'quiver' is used here in Book 5:

A Long Way Down

Jack sat down with a bump. His mouth turned down and his bottom lip began to <u>quiver</u>. "Stay strong, baby boy," whispered Erin as she hugged him.

'quiver' means: shake or tremble

Circle the word or phrase that could be replaced with the word 'quiver' in the following text:

> The ball crashed into the goal. It came at such a speed that the goalpost started to shake where the ball had slammed into it.

Can you write two different sentences of your own using the word 'quiver'?

1.

_____

_____

2.

_____

_____

Book 5: Character profile

Use the word bank to help you describe baby Jack.

milkshake   little   chasing Erin   cake

animals   sleeping   playing   train set

splashing in the waves

Name _____

Age _____

Appearance _____

Loves _____

Hates *Being hungry makes Jack frown!!*
_____

Hobbies _____

Favorite food _____

This is a writing frame to help structure creative writing. Ask the student to use words from the word bank to help them create a character profile for Jack. They will know some things from the story, but encourage them to be creative in their answers and to try to write in full sentences, using capital letters and full stops.
This sheet may be photocopied by the purchaser. © Phonic Books Ltd 2015

Book 5: Stepping stones reading game 'ow' and 'oi' words

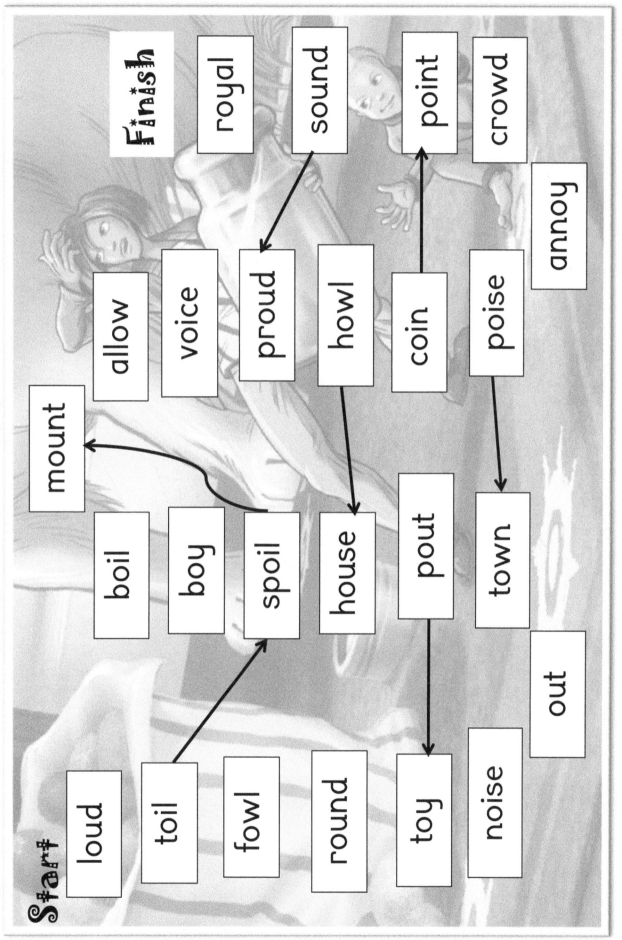

Start loud, toil, fowl, round, toy, noise, out, town, pout, coin, howl, spoil, house, boy, boil, mount, allow, voice, proud, poise, annoy, crowd, point, sound, royal **Finish**

A game for 1-4 players: Play with counters and dice.
Players should read aloud the words that they land on at the end of each turn and follow the direction arrows if they land on them.
This sheet may be photocopied by the purchaser. © Phonic Books Ltd 2015

Book 5: Spelling assessment for words with 'ow' and 'oi' spellings

1.

ow	**ou**	**oy**	**oi**
cow	out	boy	coin
down	pout	toy	spoil
clown	sound	royal	point

2.

ow	**ou**	**oy**	**oi**
power	loudest	oyster	avoid
towel	voucher	annoy	toilet
howling	mouthful	employ	ointment

These lists can be used as a spelling assessment at the end of each book. The teacher can add words from list 2 for students who are ready for that stage. When dictating a word, first say the word on its own. Next, say a sentence with the word in it (to put the word in the context of a sentence) and then repeat the word. This ensures that the student has heard the word correctly, e.g. "Fainted. The boy fainted when he saw the mouse. Fainted."

Book 6: A Gruesome Monster

Contents

* 7 things that are not true:
Ziggy, the cat, had not been taken into the space game; Erin did not press a flashing green button; freezing snow did not fill the spaceship; the monster did not want Erin to drive the spaceship to his planet; Erin and Jack could not make themselves invisible; Erin did not feed Jack a mound of apple chunks; Erin did not have energy cells on her elbow.

Book 6: Blending and segmenting: 'oo'

too	t	oo		
you				
rude		u		e
chew				
truth				
clue				
boot				
soup				
threw				
rule				
proof				
cruel				
flute				

Blend the sounds into a word. Segment the word into sounds by writing one sound in each square.
Split vowel spellings (u–e) are represented by half squares linked together.
This sheet may be photocopied by the purchaser. © Phonic Books Ltd 2015

Book 6: Reading and sorting words with 'oo' spellings

oo	ou	ue	u-e	ew	u

pool	rude	blue	group
grew	July	shoot	youth
flew	rule	true	brutal
glue	scoop	crude	chew
route	judo	smooth	sue
brute	jewel	include	plume
shampoo	scuba	coupon	flume
drew	proof	loose	crew

Book 6: Reading and spelling words with 'oo' spellings

oo	ou	ue
___	___	___
___	___	___
___	___	___
___	___	___
___	___	___

u-e	ew	u
___	___	___
___	___	___
___	___	___

pool   rude   group   grew   blue   brutal   shoot
youth   true   rule   flew   judo   smooth   coupon
brute   chew   July   glue   shampoo   route
gruesome   soup   scoop   clue

List the words according to the 'oo' spellings.

Book 6: Timed reading of words with 'oo' spellings

pool   rude   group   grew   blue   brutal   shoot
youth   true   rule   flew   judo   smooth   coupon
brute   chew   July   glue   shampoo   route
gruesome   soup   scoop   clue   too   you   to
truth   boot   threw   super   cruel   flute

1st try   **Time:**

- -

pool   rude   group   grew   blue   brutal   shoot
youth   true   rule   flew   judo   smooth   coupon
brute   chew   July   glue   shampoo   route
gruesome   soup   scoop   clue   too   you   to
truth   boot   threw   super   cruel   flute

2nd try   **Time:**

- -

pool   rude   group   grew   blue   brutal   shoot
youth   true   rule   flew   judo   smooth   coupon
brute   chew   July   glue   shampoo   route
gruesome   soup   scoop   clue   too   you   to
truth   boot   threw   super   cruel   flute

3rd try   **Time:**

Book 6: Chunking two-syllable words with 'oo'

bamboo	bam	boo	bamboo
youthful			
chewing			
truthful			
clueless			
include			
scooter			
coupon			
Andrew			
brutal			
gruesome			
intrude			
tattoo			
salute			

Split the word into two syllables. Write each syllable in a box.
Write the whole word while saying the syllables.

98

Book 6: Phonic patterns

Color in the words with 'oo' spellings.

scoop	truthful	humble	intrude
youthful	clueless	coupon	culminate
hungry	include	Andrew	tattoo
chewing	scooter	brutal	salute
underneath	buttercup	gruesome	bamboo

Fold this sheet on the dotted line. Read the words in the column on the left. Listen to the sounds in the words. Color in the boxes with words that have 'oo' spellings. Repeat this in the other columns. Unfold the sheet and check the correct words have been colored in. This sheet may be photocopied by the purchaser. © Phonic Books Ltd 2015

Book 6: Reading and sorting words with <oo> spelling

look	moon

food	hood	tool	drool
cook	fool	scoop	hook
school	mood	good	wood
moon	spoon	ooze	took
room	crook	groom	stool
wool	root	foot	book
noon	shook	boot	brook
cool	balloon	woof	stood

Photocopy this page onto card and cut out the words. Read and sort the cards out according to the sounds of the <oo> spelling. The two sounds are l'oo'k and m'oo'n. This sheet may be photocopied by the purchaser. © Phonic Books Ltd 2015

Book 6: Phonic patterns

Color in the words with the sound 'oo' as in 'moon'.

scoop	hoop	took	tool
soon	loop	tattoo	cook
book	noon	scooter	drool
balloon	food	groom	room
look	good	cool	spoon

Fold this sheet on the dotted line. Read the words in the column on the left. Listen to the sounds in the words. Color in the boxes with words that have 'oo' spellings as it sounds in the word m'oo'n. Repeat this in the other columns. Unfold the sheet and check the correct words have been colored in. This sheet may be photocopied by the purchaser. © Phonic Books Ltd 2015

Book 6: Is it true?

Erin and baby Jack had been taken into the space game with Ziggy, the cat!

They were in a spaceship. Erin pressed a flashing green button and a burst of freezing snow filled the ship!

A space monster was looming over the spaceship. He wanted Erin to drive the ship to his planet.

Erin and Jack escaped from the spaceship and the monster. They were amazed to find they had magic powers – they could make themselves invisible!

Erin and Jack flew away and landed on a planet made completely of food. Erin fed Jack a mound of apple chunks.

They needed to get out of the game. Erin was afraid they were running out of energy as she only had three energy cells left on her elbow.

There are 7 things in the story above that are not true. Can you spot them?

Ask the student to read the text carefully and circle any false information that has been planted in the story.

Book 6: Picture the scene

The spaceship has flames shooting from behind it.

There is a huge monster on top of the spaceship.

Erin and Jack are floating in space next to the ship.

There is a big planet in one corner.

There is a cluster of seven stars in the sky.

Book 6: Dictation

Erin and Jack found themselves in a spaceship in the space game! Jack was __ __ ___ __ __ ___, but Erin needed to look for __ __ ___ __ to help them escape.

When Erin pressed a button, a freezing cold wind __ __ ___ them across the __ ___ __.

A __ __ ___some monster was ___ ___ __ ___ on the spaceship. He wanted to destroy the two of them.

They escaped the __ __ __ __ monster and the spaceship and found themselves floating in space. They had super powers!

Erin and Jack __ __ ___ to a planet made of __ ___ __.

They ate some soft __ ___ __ ___ __ and rested under a __ __ ___ __ of __ __ ___ __ ___ __ __. They needed __ __ escape the __ ___ __ planet and reach the planet of __ ___ __ __ __.

Erin and Jack found themselves in a spaceship in the space game! Jack was **s n oo z i ng**, but Erin needed to look for **c l ue s** to help them escape.
When Erin pressed a button, a freezing cold wind **b l ew** them across the **r oo m**.
A **g r ue**some monster was **ch ew ing** on the spaceship. He wanted to destroy the two of them.
They escaped the **r u d e** monster and the spaceship and found themselves floating in space. They had super powers!
Erin and Jack **f l ew** to a planet made of **f oo d**.
They ate some soft **n oo d le s** and rested under a **g r ou p** of **m u sh r oo m s**. They needed **t o** escape the **f oo d** planet and reach the planet of **j ew e l s**.

Use the text at the bottom of the page for dictation. The section for dictation can either be cut off by the teacher or folded along the dotted line to allow the student to self-check their spellings on completion. Dictate the passage to the student. Ask her/him to spell the missing words, writing a sound on each line. Explain that longer lines indicate spellings with more than one letter, e.g. s ea
This sheet may be photocopied by the purchaser. © Phonic Books Ltd 2015

Book 6: Punctuation activity

Capital letters, full stops and speech marks

Remember you will need to use capital letters and an exclamation mark <u>inside</u> your speech marks.

they landed with a bump under a spotted toadstool jack was feeling hungry erin scooped up a handful of soft noodles to feed him if we stay much longer, we can make noodle soup! she joked

There are 4 capital letters, 4 full stops and 1 set of speech marks missing.

Did you spot them all?

Ask the student to read through the text and add in capital letters, full stops and speech marks where necessary. Encourage the student to read aloud as this will help him/her identify where the sentences stop.

Book 6: Developing vocabulary: gruesome

The word 'gruesome' is used here in Book 6:

A _gruesome_ space monster loomed over the spaceship. His cruel voice boomed across the galaxy. "You fools have set me free! I am free to destroy you two and every living thing on this planet."

'gruesome' means: horrific and causing great distress

Circle the word or phrase that could be replaced with the word 'gruesome' in the following text:

Leo and I went to see a film for his birthday. I had to cover my face when the monster was doing disgusting things to his enemy.

Can you write two different sentences of your own using the word 'gruesome'?

1.

_____

_____

2.

_____

_____

Book 6: Character profile

Use the word bank to help you describe the gruesome monster.

```
teeth          destruction      purple          scales
eating metal            fighting       evil eyes    claws
              jaws
```

Name _____

Age _____

Loves _____

Hates _____

Hobbies *The gruesome monster is very keen to destroy every living thing on the planet!*
_____

Favorite food _____

This is a writing frame to help structure creative writing. Ask the student to use words from the word bank to help them create a character profile for the gruesome monster. They will know some things from the story, but encourage them to be creative in their answers and to try to write in full sentences, using capital letters and full stops. This framework can also be used as a planning document for a piece of free writing.

107

Book 6: Stepping stones reading game 'oo' words

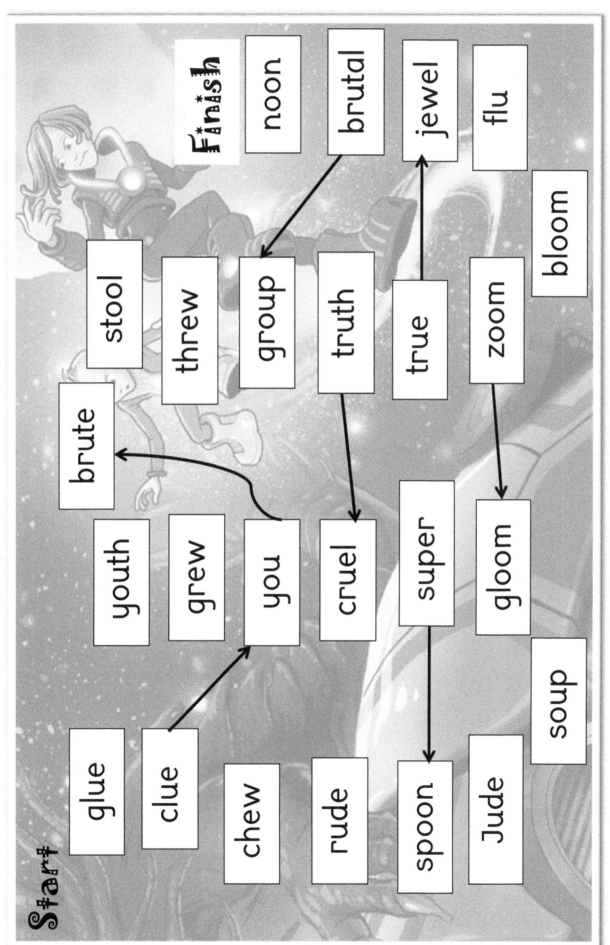

Start

glue
clue
chew
rude

youth
grew
you
cruel
super
spoon
Jude
soup
gloom
zoom

brute
stool
threw
group
truth
true
jewel
flu
bloom

Finish
noon
brutal

A game for 1–4 players: Play with counters and dice.
Players should read aloud the words that they land on at the end of each turn and follow the direction arrows if they land on them.
This sheet may be photocopied by the purchaser. © Phonic Books Ltd 2015

108

Book 6: Spelling assessment for words with 'oo' spellings

1.

oo	ou	ew	ue	u-e	u
too	you	grew	true	rude	truth
soon	soup	flew	blue	rule	July
cool	youth	drew	glue	brute	super

2.

oo	ou	ew	ue	u-e
swoop	group	chew	clueless	include
scoop	coupon	threw	cruel	conclude
foolish	route	screw	gruesome	delude

These lists can be used as a spelling assessment at the end of each book. The teacher can add words from list 2 for students who are ready for that stage. When dictating a word, first say the word on its own. Next, say a sentence with the word in it (to put the word in the context of a sentence) and then repeat the word. This ensures that the student has heard the word correctly, e.g. "Fainted. The boy fainted when he saw the mouse. Fainted." © Phonic Books Ltd 2015

This sheet may be photocopied by the purchaser.

Book 7: Time is Running Out!
Contents

* 6 things that are not true:
Erin and Jack did not need to find a golden slice of apple pie; the giant cupcake did not try to eat Jack; the cakes were not getting ready for a long-distance bike ride; cold rain did not sweep the icing off Erin and Jack; the striped cake was not hit by a cherry pie: they are not off to the planet of pets.

Book 7: Blending and segmenting: 'ie'

light	l	igh	t		
tie					
fine		i		e	
by					
mind					
bright					
drive					
China					
fries					
shine					
tonight					
slimy					
tried					

Blend the sounds into a word. Segment the word into sounds by writing one sound in each square.
Split vowel spellings (i–e) are represented by half squares linked together.
This sheet may be photocopied by the purchaser. © Phonic Books Ltd 2015

Book 7: Reading and sorting words with 'ie' spellings

igh	ie	i-e	i	y

shy	thigh	slime	invite
final	try	mine	high
life	dried	kite	slight
find	line	why	die
kind	dive	spies	nice
bright	lying	behind	fright
knife	shine	mile	style
giant	idol	midnight	flies

Photocopy this page onto card and cut out the words. Read and sort the cards out according to the 'ie' headings at the top of the page.

Book 7: Reading and spelling words with 'ie' spellings

igh	ie	i-e
_____	_____	_____
_____	_____	_____
_____	_____	_____
_____	_____	_____

y	i
_____	_____
_____	_____
_____	_____

final   behind   try   high   bright   dried   kite   dive
spies   why   flies   shy   shine   lying   mine   slight
kind   midnight   die   mind

Book 7: Timed reading of words with 'ie' spellings

final	try	mine	high	life	dried	kite	slight
find	line	why	die	kind	dive	spies	nice
bright	behind	fright	knife	shine	mile	style	
giant	wife	midnight	flies	shy	thigh	slime	

invite spite tonight

1st try   **Time:**

----

final	try	mine	high	life	dried	kite	slight
find	line	why	die	kind	dive	spies	nice
bright	behind	fright	knife	shine	mile	style	
giant	wife	midnight	flies	shy	thigh	slime	

invite spite tonight

2nd try   **Time:**

----

final	try	mine	high	life	dried	kite	slight
find	line	why	die	kind	dive	spies	nice
bright	behind	fright	knife	shine	mile	style	
giant	wife	midnight	flies	shy	thigh	slime	

invite spite tonight

3rd try   **Time:**

Book 7: Chunking two-syllable words with 'ie'

word	syllable 1	syllable 2	whole word
inside	in	side	inside
sunlight			
slimy			
magpie			
reply			
spicy			
dryer			
twilight			
decide			
denied			
bible			
rely			
delight			
beside			

Split the word into two syllables. Write each syllable in a box.
Write the whole word while saying the syllables.

116

Book 7: Phonic patterns

Color in the words with 'ie' spellings.

minted	tight	crying	hungry
splinter	king	magpie	spine
sunlight	fishing	happy	tilted
inside	giant	midnight	side
high	glitter	knife	kind

Book 7: Is it true?

Erin and Jack need to find the golden slice of apple pie to escape the food planet. Erin spots it at the end of a long line of swirling cakes. They hide behind a giant cupcake and have such a shock when the cupcake tries to eat Jack!

The cakes are getting ready to go on a long distance bike ride. Erin and Jack disguise themselves as a cake so they can join in.

As they are running along, a sudden burst of cold rain sweeps the icing disguise off them. A striped cake stops to help. He tugs them along behind him in the sky like kites.

Disaster strikes when the striped cake is hit by a cherry pie. Luckily, the game is saved when Danny joins the game from the outside!

Danny mends the striped cake and helps them win the race. Erin and Jack have the golden slice of cake. Now they are ready to enter the next level. They are off to the planet of pets.

There are 6 things in the story above that are not true. Can you spot them?

Ask the student to read the text carefully and circle any false information that has been planted in the story.

Book 7: Picture the scene

Erin and Jack are floating in the sky behind Stripe, the cake.

There are three lollipop trees next to them.

The road underneath Stripe has a striped pattern.

There are lots of round candies in the sky.

Erin is holding the golden slice!

Book 7: Dictation

Erin and Jack needed to _ _ _ _ the golden _ _ _ _ _
of cake to win the game.

Erin spotted the cake at the end of a long _ _ _ _ of cakes
waiting to race. She and Jack grabbed a sheet of _ _ _ ___
to use as a disguise.

The _ _ _ ___ was tugged off them by the wind.
A _ _ _ _ cake, with _ _ _ _ _ _ _, stopped to help
them. He tugged them along, _ ___ up in the _ _ _ like
_ _ _ _ _! Sadly, an apple _ ___ crashed into Stripe!

Luckily, Danny was at home, playing the game! He helped to
mend Stripe. Erin and Jack won the race. The _ _ _ _ _ was
the golden _ _ _ _ _!

It was _ _ _ _ to escape this level and leave the planet of
food. The next planet was the _ _ _ _ _ level of the game!

Erin and Jack needed to **f i n d** the golden **s l i c e** of cake to win the game.
Erin spotted the cake at the end of a long **l i n e** of cakes waiting to race. She and Jack grabbed a
sheet of **i c i ng** to use as a disguise.
The **i c i ng** was tugged off them by the wind. A **t i n y** cake with **s t r i p e s** stopped to help them. He
tugged them along, **h igh** up in the **s k y** like **k i t e s**! Sadly, an apple **p ie** crashed into Stripe!
Luckily, Danny was at home, playing the game! He helped to mend Stripe. Erin and Jack won the race.
The **p r i z e** was the golden **s l i c e**!
It was **t i m e** to escape this level and leave the planet of food. The next planet was the **f i n a l** level
of the game!

Use the text at the bottom of the page for dictation. The section for dictation can either be cut off
by the teacher or folded along the dotted line to allow the student to self-check their spellings on
completion. Dictate the passage to the student. Ask her/him to spell the missing words, writing a
sound on each line. Explain that longer lines indicate spellings with more than one letter, e.g. s ea

Book 7: Punctuation activity

Capital letters, full stops and exclamation marks

Exclamation marks are used at the end of a sentence that is particularly unusual or exciting. Reading the text aloud, with expression, will help you decide where it would be useful to use one.

the cakes lined up it was a tight fit and erin had to fight for a space she and jack sped off suddenly, the sheet of icing was tugged off them by a gust of wind

There are 6 capital letters, 3 full stops and 1 exclamation mark missing.

Did you spot them all?

Ask the student to read through the text and add in capital letters, full stops and exclamation mark where necessary. Encourage the student to read aloud as this will help him/her identify where the sentences stop.

Book 7: Developing vocabulary: gurgled

The word 'gurgled' is used here in Book 7:

Suddenly, a shadow fell over the race and a giant face filled the sky. Erin was terrified, but Jack giggled with delight and gurgled, "Dan Dan". Danny was outside the screen, gazing in!

'gurgled' means: to make a low, bubbling noise

Circle the word or phrase that could be replaced with the word 'gurgled' in the following text:

The smell of roast chicken was amazing. Tom sniffed the air. His tummy made low grumbling noises. He was so hungry.

Can you write two different sentences of your own using the word 'gurgled'?

1.
_____

_____

2.
_____

_____

Book 7: Character profile

Use the word bank to help you describe Stripe, the cake.

racing

helping

kind

competitions

buttercream

fast

hurt

running

exercise

Name _____

Age _____

Loves _____

Hates _____

Hobbies _____

Favorite food _____ Stripe loves anything sweet! _____

This is a writing frame to help structure creative writing. Ask the student to use words from the word bank to help them create a character profile for Stripe, the cake. They will know some things from the story, but encourage them to be creative in their answers and to try to write in full sentences, using capital letters and full stops. This framework can also be used as a planning document for a piece of free writing.

Book 7: Stepping stones reading game 'ie' words

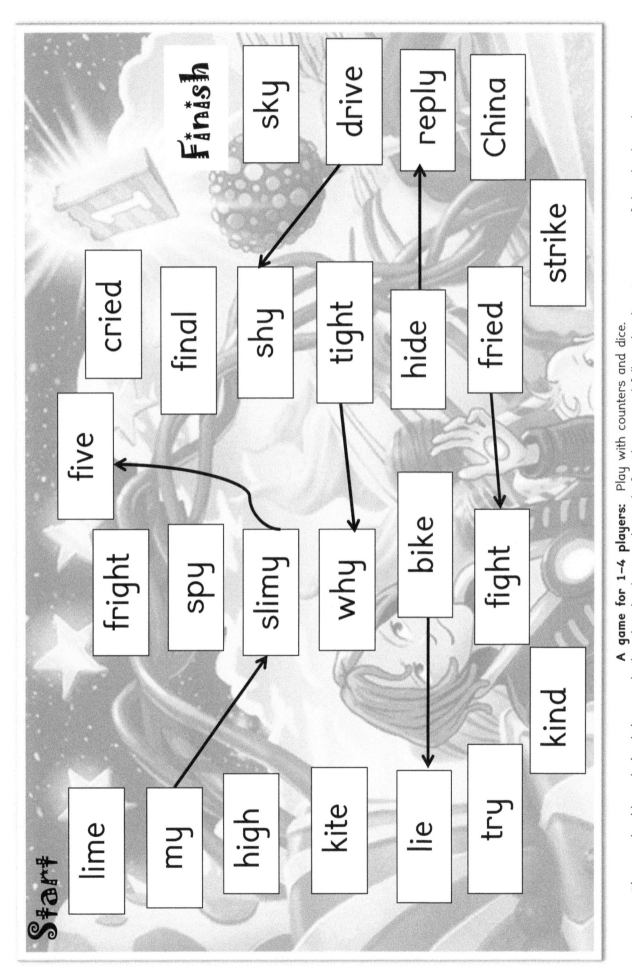

Start

Finish

lime	cried	sky	
my	final	drive	reply
high	shy		China
kite	tight	hide	strike
lie		fried	
try	why	bike	
	slimy		fight
spy			kind
fright			
five			

A game for 1–4 players: Play with counters and dice.

Players should read aloud the words that they land on at the end of each turn and follow the direction arrows if they land on them.
This sheet may be photocopied by the purchaser. © Phonic Books Ltd 2015

124

Book 7: Spelling assessment for words with 'ie' spellings

1.

igh	**ie**	**i-e**	**y**	**i**
light	tie	time	my	find
might	die	life	by	wild
tight	pie	hide	fly	final

2.

igh	**ie**	**i-e**	**y**	**i**
flight	cried	glide	dying	spider
fright	tried	smile	trying	giant
tonight	spied	stripe	crying	behind

These lists can be used as a spelling assessment at the end of each book. The teacher can add words from list 2 for students who are ready for that stage. When dictating a word, first say the word on its own. Next, say a sentence with the word in it (to put the word in the context of a sentence) and then repeat the word. This ensures that the student has heard the word correctly, e.g. "Fainted. The boy fainted when he saw the mouse. Fainted."

Book 8: An Awful Planet
Contents

* 7 things that are not true:
The planet of jewels was not freezing cold; Danny did not tell Erin to use a magic lantern; Erin and Jack did not throw water over the jewels; Danny did not tell them to find a golden necklace; Erin did not find something at the bottom of a stream; Erin did not crash into Danny's elbow; Danny did not let Jack travel in his hat.

Book 8: Blending and segmenting: aw, awe, a, al, au, ough spellings

all	a	ll		
saw				
haunt				
fought				
walk				
small				
straw				
halt				
August				
talk				
thought				
yawn				
awe				

Blend the sounds into a word. Segment the word into sounds by writing one sound in each square.

Book 8: Reading and sorting words with aw, awe, a, al, au, ough spellings

aw	**awe**	**a**	**al**

au	**ough**

yawn	vault	tall	jaw
fought	Paul	halt	awesome
hawk	author	call	thaw
haunt	thought	stalk	draw
sought	fault	almost	haul
haunt	straw	stall	paw
applaud	awe	awful	talk

Book 8: Reading and spelling words with a, aw and awe spellings

a	aw	awe
_____	_____	_____
_____	_____	_____
_____	_____	
_____	_____	
_____	_____	
_____	_____	
_____	_____	
_____	_____	
	_____	

call   claw   small   draw   all   saw   stall   straw
ball   bawl   awe   dawn   awesome   jaw   fall
crawl   halt   hawk   shawl   scald

List the words according to the spellings.
This sheet may be photocopied by the purchaser. © Phonic Books Ltd 2015

Book 8: Reading and spelling words with al, au and ough spellings

al	au	ough
_____	_____	_____
_____	_____	_____
_____	_____	_____
_____	_____	_____
	_____	_____
	_____	_____
	_____	_____
	_____	
	_____	

ought   haul   walk   fought   August   faucet   sought
fault   talk   bought   maul   author   chalk   brought
launch   thought   haunt   stalk   nought   assault

List the words according to spellings.

Book 8: Timed reading of words with aw, awe, a, al, au, ough spellings

tall   fought   call   halt   awesome   haunt   thought
stalk   draw   almost   walk   August   claw   stall
paw   awful   talk   yawn   chalk   bought   scald
shawl   malt   small   thought   awe   faucet   hawk
brought   fault

1st try	Time:	

tall   fought   call   halt   awesome   haunt   thought
stalk   draw   almost   walk   August   claw   stall
paw   awful   talk   yawn   chalk   bought   scald
shawl   malt   small   thought   awe   faucet   hawk
brought   fault

2nd try	Time:	

tall   fought   call   halt   awesome   haunt   thought
stalk   draw   almost   walk   August   claw   stall
paw   awful   talk   yawn   chalk   bought   scald
shawl   malt   small   thought   awe   faucet   hawk
brought   fault

3rd try	Time:	

This timed reading activity is for the student to improve his/her reading speed and fluency. Ask the student to read the words as fast as he/she can. Record the time in the box. Repeat the activity. This sheet can be cut or folded along the dotted lines to allow for different presentations.
This sheet may be photocopied by the purchaser. © Phonic Books Ltd 2015

Book 8: Chunking two-syllable words with aw, awe, a, al, au, ough spellings

	aw	ful	awful
awful			
assault			
seesaw			
almost			
haunted			
scalded			
thoughtful			
talking			
faultless			
squawking			
calling			
August			
lawful			
awesome			

Split the word into two syllables. Write each syllable in a box.
Write the whole word while saying the syllables.
This sheet may be photocopied by the purchaser. © Phonic Books Ltd 2015

Book 8: Phonic patterns

Color in the words with aw, awe, a, al, au, ough spellings.

awe	hawk	dragon	thought
happy	card	claw	bald
tall	author	walk	kitten
awesome	brought	talk	applaud
pleased	farmyard	butter	haunt

Fold this sheet on the dotted line. Read the words in the column on the left. Listen to the sounds in the words. Color in the boxes with words that have aw, awe, a, al, au, ough spellings. Repeat this in the other columns. Unfold the sheet and check the correct words have been colored in. This sheet may be photocopied by the purchaser. © Phonic Books Ltd 2015

Book 8: Is it true?

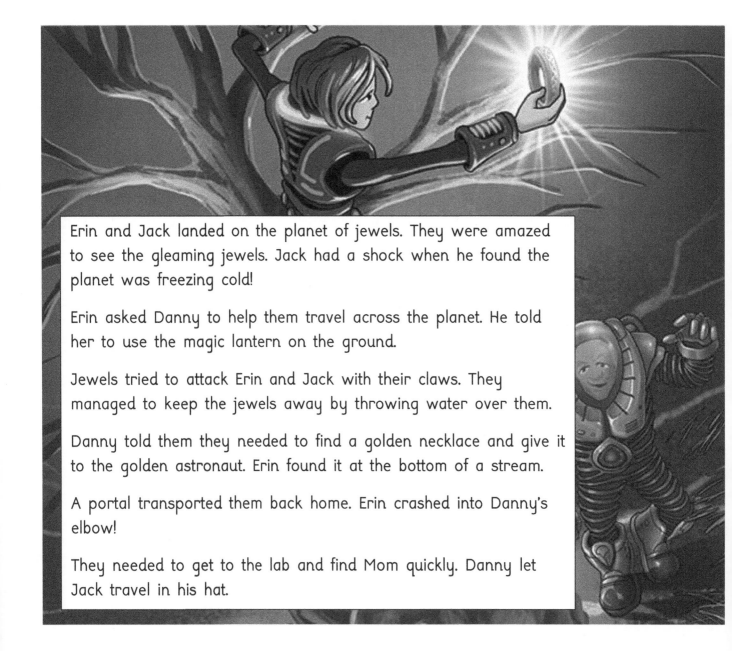

Erin and Jack landed on the planet of jewels. They were amazed to see the gleaming jewels. Jack had a shock when he found the planet was freezing cold!

Erin asked Danny to help them travel across the planet. He told her to use the magic lantern on the ground.

Jewels tried to attack Erin and Jack with their claws. They managed to keep the jewels away by throwing water over them.

Danny told them they needed to find a golden necklace and give it to the golden astronaut. Erin found it at the bottom of a stream.

A portal transported them back home. Erin crashed into Danny's elbow!

They needed to get to the lab and find Mom quickly. Danny let Jack travel in his hat.

There are 7 things in the story above that are not true. Can you spot them?

Book 8: Picture the scene

Erin is sitting in Danny's hat.

Danny is riding his skateboard.

Behind him is a huge bush and a brick wall.

There is an apple core on the path near him.

Book 8: Dictation

The planet of jewels was an ___ __ __ __, toxic place! Jack had sore hands from __ __ ___ __ __ ___ on the scorching surface.

Erin used a magic torch to __ __ ___ a safe path away from the jewels. The jewels snapped at them with their __ ___ __. They tried to __ ___ __ them with __ __ ___ __ like animal __ ___ __!

The golden __ __ __ __ __ __ ___ __ was like a lord in the game. Danny helped them find him a golden ring.
The __ __ __ __ __ __ ___ __ opened a portal and transported them back home.

Erin was so glad to have escaped, but she was sad they were still so __ __ __ ___.

They set off for the lab to find Mom. They had to find her before __ ___ __ __ __ ___.

The planet of jewels was an **aw f u l**, toxic place! Jack had sore hands from **c r aw l i ng** on the scorching surface.

Erin used a magic torch to **d r aw** a safe path away from the jewels. The jewels snapped at them with their **j aw s**. They tried to **m au l** them with **c l aw s** like animal **p aw s**!

The golden **a s t r o n au t** was like a lord in the game. Danny helped them find him a golden ring. The **a s t r o n au t** opened a portal and transported them back home.

Erin was so glad to have escaped, but she was sad they were still so **s m all**.

They set off for the lab to find Mom. They had to find her before **n igh t f a ll**.

Book 8: Punctuation activity

Capital letters, full stops and exclamation marks

Exclamation marks are used at the end of sentences that are particularly unusual or exciting. Reading the text aloud, with expression, will help you decide where it would be useful to use an exclamation mark.

the planet was scorching hot erin grabbed jack and blew on his hands before they got sore a swarm of small jewels formed around them, snapping their jaws

There are 4 capital letters, 1 full stop and 2 exclamation marks missing.

Did you spot them all?

Ask the student to read through the text and add in capital letters, full stops and exclamation marks where necessary. Encourage the student to read aloud as this will help him/her identify where the sentences stop.

Book 8: Developing vocabulary: toxic

The word 'toxic' is used here in Book 8:

> They ran along the path. More jewels tried to maul them with claws like wild animal paws. Erin did not want a war. She just wanted to escape from this <u>toxic</u> planet.

'toxic' means: harmful or deadly

Circle the word or phrase that could be replaced with the word 'toxic' in the following text:

> Jack had made Mom a magical supper. He had used a blue food dye in the mashed potato. Mom took a deep breath. She wanted to be kind, but the glowing blue mash really looked as if it might kill her.

Can you write two different sentences of your own using the word 'toxic'?

1.

_____

_____

2.

_____

_____

Book 8: Character profile

Use the word bank to help you describe the jewel monster.

snapping jaws

swarm

torment

humans

animal claws

chasing

spiky

evil

maul

Name _____

Age _____

Loves _____

Hates _The jewel monster hates visitors to his planet!_
_____

Hobbies _____

Favorite food _____

Book 8: Stepping stones reading game: aw, awe, a, al, au, ough words

Start

Finish

haul	scald
claw	crawl
drawn	stall
	bought
talk	
all	fall
paw	

stalk

hawk — law

small — maul

raw — call

wall — fault

draw — saw

awe — haunt

fought

A game for 1–4 players: Play with counters and dice.
Players should read aloud the words that they land on at the end of each turn and follow the direction arrows if they land on them.
This sheet may be photocopied by the purchaser. © Phonic Books Ltd 2015

Book 8: Spelling assessment for words with aw, awe, a, al, au, ough spellings

ough
fought
thought
brought

al
walk
talk
chalk

awe
awe
awesome

aw
saw
claw
draw
hawk
awful

au
maul
haunt
August
launch
fault

a
all
call
almost
halt
scald

These lists can be used as a spelling assessment at the end of each book. The teacher may want to offer this test in two halves as there are so many spellings. When dictating a word, first say the word on its own. Next, say a sentence with the word in it (to put the word in the context of a sentence) and then repeat the word. This ensures that the student has heard the word correctly, e.g. "Fainted. The boy fainted when he saw the mouse. Fainted."

Book 9: No Time to Spare
Contents

* 12 things that are not true:
Danny did not let Jack ride in his hat; Jack did not cry all the way to the lab; Danny did not give Jack a candy to eat; Erin did not jump out of Danny's hat when they got to the lab; the little girl did not find Erin at the top of the stairs; the antidote did not taste like plums; Jack was not happy to take the antidote; Polly did not give Erin a plate of grapes; Polly did not put a leaf in Erin's hair; Polly did not go off to a party; Erin did not hold onto a kite and fly out of the window; it was not the middle of the night when Erin left Polly's home.

144

Book 9: Blending and segmenting: air, are, ear, ere, eir spellings

fair	f	air				
care						
their						
pear						
chair						
share						
where						
swear						
stair						
spare						
beware						
careless						
werewolf						

Blend the sounds into a word. Segment the word into sounds by writing one sound in each square.
This sheet may be photocopied by the purchaser. © Phonic Books Ltd 2015

Book 9: Reading and sorting words with air, are, ear, ere, eir spellings

air	are	ear	ere	eir

fare	chair	rare	swear
pair	blare	wear	there
heir	lair	stare	bear
mare	flair	tear	dare
where	their	bare	pear
spare	affair	fair	declare
despair	care	stare	impair
hare	glare	Clair	fairly

Book 9: Reading and spelling words with air, are, ear, ere, eir spellings

air	are	ear
_____	_____	_____
_____	_____	_____
_____	_____	_____
_____	_____	_____
_____	_____	_____

ere	eir
_____	_____
_____	

air   bare   bear   there   their   fair   chair
dare   pear   share   tear   stair   glare   spare
wear   swear   despair   where

List the words according to their spellings.

148

Book 9: Timed reading of words with air, are, ear, ere, eir spellings

air   bare   there   heir   pear   chair   care
where   flare   wear   their   ware   stair   fare
beware   lair   scare   tear   mare   Clair   fair
spare   despair   bear   share   repair   swear
declare   glare   dairy   rare   hairy

1st try	Time:

air   bare   there   heir   pear   chair   care
where   flare   wear   their   ware   stair   fare
beware   lair   scare   tear   mare   Clair   fair
spare   despair   bear   share   repair   swear
declare   glare   dairy   rare   hairy

2nd try	Time:

air   bare   there   heir   pear   chair   care
where   flare   wear   their   ware   stair   fare
beware   lair   scare   tear   mare   Clair   fair
spare   despair   bear   share   repair   swear
declare   glare   dairy   rare   hairy

3rd try	Time:

This timed reading activity is for the student to improve his/her reading speed and fluency. Ask the student to read the words as fast as he/she can. Record the time in the box. Repeat the activity. This sheet can be cut or folded along the dotted lines to allow for different presentations. This sheet may be photocopied by the purchaser. © Phonic Books Ltd 2015

149

Book 9: Chunking two-syllable words with air, are, ear, ere, eir spellings

fairly	fair	ly	fairly
beware			
nowhere			
farewell			
despair			
affair			
careless			
rarely			
heirloom			
hairless			
repair			
declare			
footwear			
unfair			

Split the word into two syllables. Write each syllable in a box.
Write the whole word while saying the syllables.
This sheet may be photocopied by the purchaser. © Phonic Books Ltd 2015

Book 9: Phonic patterns

Color in the words with air, are, ear, ere, eir spellings.

pain	fair	spare	nail
where	great	despair	unfair
care	statement	trade	bear
tray	their	where	claim
stairs	pear	there	dare

Fold this sheet on the dotted line. Read the words in the column on the left. Listen to the sounds in the words. Color in the boxes with words that have air, are, ear, ere, eir spellings. Repeat this in the other columns. Unfold the sheet and check the correct words have been colored in. This sheet may be photocopied by the purchaser. © Phonic Books Ltd 2015

Book 9: Is it true?

Danny raced to the lab with Erin and baby Jack both riding in his hat. Baby Jack was so hungry that he cried all the way. Danny gave him a candy to eat.

Erin jumped out of Danny's hat when they arrived at the lab. She was found, by a little girl, at the top of the stairs.

Mom gave Jack the antidote to reverse the shrinking. The antidote tasted like plums, which made Jack very happy.

The little girl made Erin into a fairy. She gave her a pair of wings and a plate of grapes. She put a leaf in Erin's hair. She made Erin a home in her doll's house before she went off to a party.

Erin escaped from the doll's house by gripping the end of a kite string and flying out of the window.

It was the middle of the night when Erin left Polly's home.

There are 12 things in the story above that are not true. Can you spot them?

Ask the student to read the text carefully and circle any false information that has been planted in the story.

Book 9: Picture the scene

Polly is holding Erin in her hand.

She has dressed Erin in fairy wings.

A doll's house is behind them.

There is a doll somewhere in the scene.

Polly has a headband, with flowers on, in her hair.

Book 9: Dictation

Danny raced to Mom's lab on his skateboard. Erin's __ ____ blew in the cold ____.

When they got ____ ____, Mom was at the top of the __ __ ____ __. Erin fell out of Danny's hat and was picked up by a little girl!

The little girl turned Erin into a __ ____ __ and gave her a chopped __ ____ to eat. Erin didn't __ ____ move.

Mom held tiny baby Jack in her hand. She gave him the antidote to make him grow. The taste made Jack __ __ ____!

Erin had to get back to the lab. She dangled a string from Polly's window and escaped into the garden. Polly had taken great __ ____ of Erin, the __ ____ __. Erin left Polly a letter from the tooth __ ____ __.

Danny raced to Mom's lab on his skateboard. Erin's **h air** blew in the cold **air**.

When they got **th ere**, Mom was at the top of the **s t air s**. Erin fell out of Danny's hat and was picked up by a little girl!

The little girl turned Erin into a **f air y** and gave her a chopped **p ear** to eat. Erin didn't **d are** move.

Mom held tiny baby Jack in her hand. She gave him the antidote to make him grow. The taste made Jack **g l are**!

Erin had to get back to the lab. She dangled a string from Polly's window and escaped into the garden. Polly had taken great **c are** of Erin, the **f air y**. Erin left Polly a letter from the tooth **f air y**.

Book 9: Punctuation activity

Speech marks

Danny and Erin raced along the street to the lab. Take care up there! yelled Danny. Erin grinned. I need some fresh air. I've had a lot of screen time this week, she said.

There are **two sets** of speech marks missing.

Did you spot them both?

Book 9: Developing vocabulary: glare

The word 'glare' is used here in Book 9:

"I used my spare key to get in. The glare was coming from the screen. I saw you when I sat down. You can spot your hair anywhere."
Erin hugged his hat. "I'm glad I have a spy for a best pal."

In this example, 'glare' means: a bright, dazzling light

Circle the word or phrase that could be replaced with the word 'glare' in the following text:

> I was in the park with my dog when I saw the spaceship land. The bright light from the headlights dazzled me. It made it hard to see, but I did not miss the green space monster stepping out of it.

Can you write two different sentences of your own using the word 'glare'?

1.

_____

_____

2.

_____

_____

Book 9: Character profile

Use the word bank to help you describe Polly.

---

playing games   doll's house   kind   caring

having fun   taking care of people   adventure

making things

Name _____

Age _____

Loves *Polly loves taking care of things!*
_____

Hates _____

Hobbies _____

Favorite food _____

This is a writing frame to help structure creative writing. Ask the student to use words from the word bank to help them create a character profile for Polly. They will know some things from the story, but encourage them to be creative in their answers and to try to write in full sentences, using capital letters and full stops. This framework can also be used as a planning document for a piece of free writing.

Book 9: Stepping stones reading game: air, are, ear, ere, eir

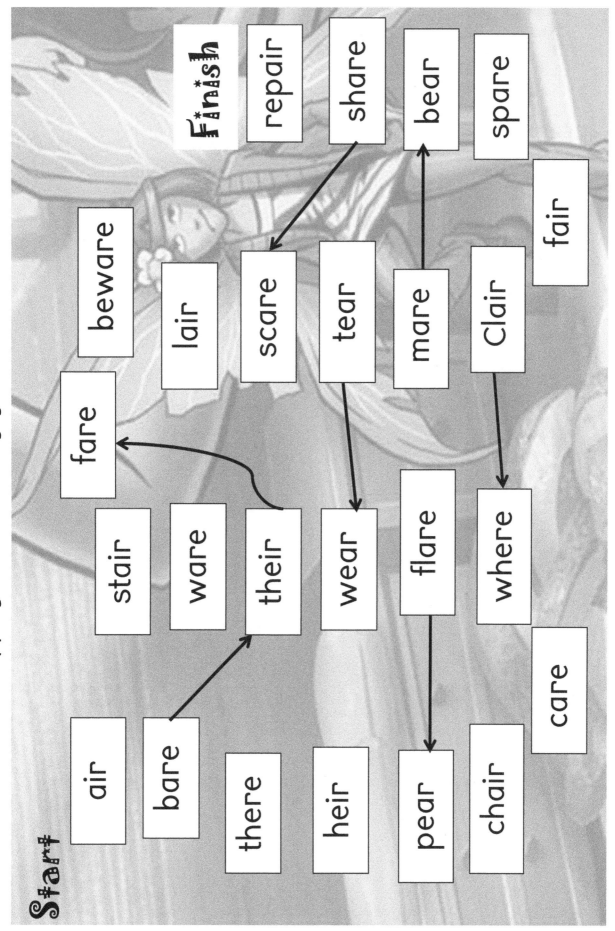

A game for 1–4 players: Play with counters and dice.

Players should read aloud the words that they land on at the end of each turn and follow the direction arrows if they land on them. This sheet may be photocopied by the purchaser. © Phonic Books Ltd 2015

Book 9: Spelling assessment for words with air, are, ear, ere, eir spellings

1.

air	are	ear	ere	eir
fair	bare	bear	there	their
chair	dare	pear	where	
stair	share	tear		

2.

air	are	ear
repair	glare	swear
unfair	compare	wearing
	unaware	bearable

These lists can be used as a spelling assessment at the end of each book. The teacher can add words from list 2 for students who are ready for that stage. When dictating a word, first say the word on its own. Next, say a sentence with the word in it (to put the word in the context of a sentence) and then repeat the word. This ensures that the student has heard the word correctly, e.g. "Fainted. The boy fainted when he saw the mouse. Fainted."

Book 10: Dark Times
Contents

* 7 things that are not true:
Erin did not escape into a sandpit; Erin did not eat some grapes she found in the grass; the loud noise was not a hot air balloon; Erin did not find the phone in a lunchbox; Erin did not ring Danny on the phone; Erin did not decide to stay small forever; Danny did not ask Erin if he could have a turn with the shrink ray.

Book 10: Blending and segmenting: ar

art	ar	t		
card				
farm				
star				
shark				
mark				
hard				
dark				
sharp				
alarm				
yard				
barbed				
darted				

Blend the sounds into a word. Segment the word into sounds by writing one sound in each square.

Book 10: Reading and sorting words with ar spelling

ar as in art	ar as in vary	ar as in warm

charm	wary	swarm	dart
harsh	yard	scary	wart
dark	arches	alarm	army
daring	stars	warn	march
staring	stark	large	war
warble	sharp	caring	harm
shark	arch	start	warthog
warlord	paring	artist	carp

Book 10: Words with ar spelling

Words with ar spelling	Page number

Book 10: Timed reading of words with ar spelling

harm   mark   shark   starve   alarm   cart
park   start   yard   harp   dark   starch
charm   harsh   arches   artist   sharp   dart
army   march   stark   farm   armor   star   art
card   shard   arches   darted

1st try   Time:

harm   mark   shark   starve   alarm   cart
park   start   yard   harp   dark   starch
charm   harsh   arches   artist   sharp   dart
army   march   stark   farm   armor   star   art
card   shard   arches   darted

2nd try   Time:

harm   mark   shark   starve   alarm   cart
park   start   yard   harp   dark   starch
charm   harsh   arches   artist   sharp   dart
army   march   stark   farm   armor   star   art
card   shard   arches   darted

3rd try   Time:

This timed reading activity is for the student to improve his/her reading speed and fluency. Ask the student to read the words as fast as he/she can. Record the time in the box. Repeat the activity. This sheet can be cut or folded along the dotted lines to allow for different presentations.

Book 10: Chunking two-syllable words with ar spelling

artist	art	ist	artist
harmful			
mustard			
armor			
marching			
darted			
barnyard			
barbed			
darkness			
custard			
darkly			
archer			
parchment			
tartan			

Book 10: Phonic patterns

Color in the words with ar spelling that sounds like ar as in art.

harm	arches	sharp	scary
harp	warn	carol	march
stark	wary	wart	farm
swarm	large	artist	cart
warble	alarm	park	dark

Fold this sheet on the dotted line. Read the words in the column on the left. Listen to the sounds in the words. Color in the boxes with words that have ar spelling like ar or in 'art'. Repeat this in the other columns. Unfold the sheet and check the correct words have been colored in. This sheet may be photocopied by the purchaser. © Phonic Books Ltd 2015

Book 10: Is it true?

Erin escaped from Polly's window into a sandpit.

She was so hungry that she ate some grapes she found in the grass. As she ran across the garden, a loud noise distracted her. It was a hot air balloon flying overhead!

Erin found a phone in an old man's lunchbox. She was able to ring Danny on the phone!

Mom was so proud of Erin for saving baby Jack. Erin decided not to take the antidote and stay small forever.

Mom locked the shrink ray away in a safe. She didn't want to risk it being used again.

Erin and Danny lay in the garden, gazing at the stars. Danny asked if next time he might have a turn with the shrink ray....

There are 7 things in the story above that are not true. Can you spot them?

Ask the student to read the text carefully and circle any false information that has been planted in the story.

Book 10: Picture the scene

Erin is running in some long grass.

The sun is shining.

There is a glass greenhouse behind Erin.

A tall flower is on the left-hand side of the scene.

A bumble bee is flying in from the right-hand side of the scene.

Book 10: Dictation

Erin had escaped from Polly's window into the __ ____ __ __ __. She was searching for a path in the long grass.

Meanwhile Danny and Mom tried to keep calm, but it was very __ ____ __. Mom's phone rang. She gasped and her heart skipped a beat when she heard Erin on the phone!

Danny raced across the __ ____ __ and met Erin at the end of the __ ____ __ __ __. He began to laugh when he saw her fairy wings! It was like a __ ____ __ __ outfit!

Mom gave Erin the antidote to make her grow. It tasted nasty!

Danny and Erin lay in the grass, looking at the stars in the night sky. Erin joked about having the chance to play the space game from inside again!

Erin had escaped from Polly's window into the **g ar d e n**. She was searching for a path in the long grass.
Meanwhile Danny and Mom tried to keep calm, but it was very **h ar d**. Mom's phone rang. She gasped and her heart skipped a beat when she heard Erin on the phone!
Danny raced across the **p ar k** and met Erin at the end of the **g ar d e n**. He began to laugh when he saw her fairy wings! It was like a **p ar t y** outfit!
Mom gave Erin the antidote to make her grow. It tasted nasty!
Danny and Erin lay in the grass, looking at the stars in the night sky. Erin joked about having the chance to play the space game from inside again!

Use the text at the bottom of the page for dictation. The section for dictation can either be cut off by the teacher or folded along the dotted line to allow the student to self-check their spellings on completion. Dictate the passage to the student. Ask her/him to spell the missing words, writing a sound on each line. Explain that longer lines indicate spellings with more than one letter, e.g. s ea

Book 10: Punctuation activity

Speech marks

Danny laughed when he saw Erin's wings and the flower in her hair! I like it, he grinned. It's a pity you can't keep it as a party outfit!

There are **two sets** of speech marks missing.

Did you spot them both?

Book 10: Developing vocabulary: shards

The word 'shards' is used here in Book 10:

Shards of bark rained down on the grass as an old man walked past with the mower. He had hit a log in the grass. When he stopped to unblock the mower, Erin spotted a phone in his jacket.

'shards' means: broken pieces of something hard

Circle the word or phrase that could be replaced with the word 'shards' in the following text:

The monster staggered across the frozen ground and loomed over them. As he raised his fist, little pieces of cold ice fell into their faces.

Can you write two different sentences of your own using the word 'shards'?

1.

_____

_____

2.

_____

_____

Book 10: Character profile

Use the word bank to help you describe Mom.

invention

protective

kind

caring

having fun

children

surfing

scientist

clever

Name _____

Age _____

Loves _____

Hates *Mom hates it when her children are having problems.*
_____

Hobbies _____

Favorite food _____

This is a writing frame to help structure creative writing. Ask the student to use words from the word bank to help them create a character profile for Mom. They will know some things from the story, but encourage them to be creative in their answers and to try to write in full sentences, using capital letters and full stops. This framework can also be used as a planning document for a piece of free writing.

Book 10: Stepping stones reading game: ar words

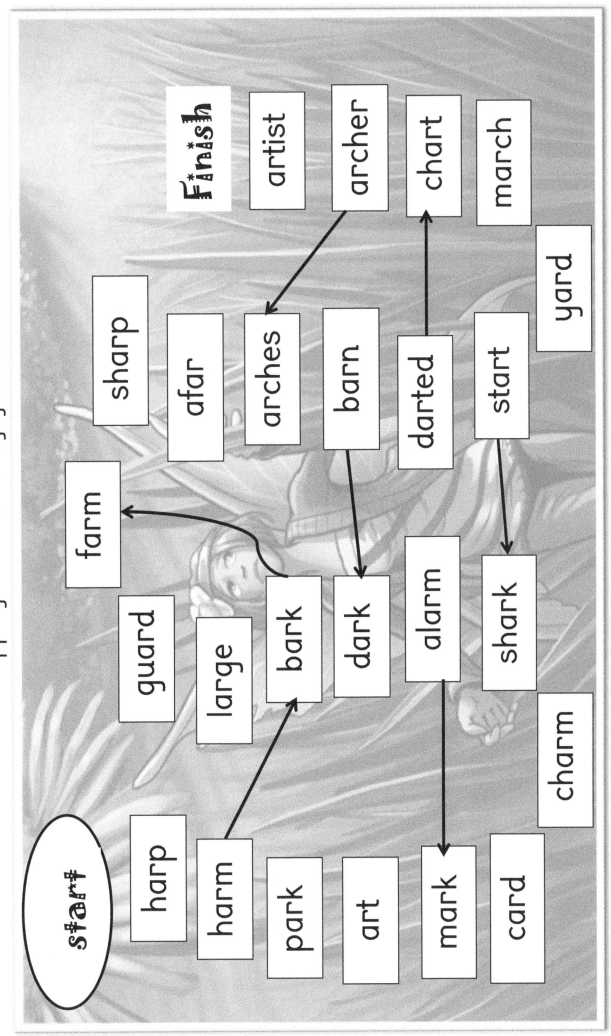

A game for 1–4 players: Play with counters and dice.
Players should read aloud the words that they land on at the end of each turn and follow the direction arrows if they land on them.
This sheet may be photocopied by the purchaser. © Phonic Books Ltd 2015

Book 10: Spelling assessment for words with ar spelling

car	dark
art	farm
ark	arch
far	part

sharp	barbed
march	charts
charm	harder
harsh	arches

These lists can be used as a spelling assessment at the end of each book. When dictating a word, first say the word on its own. Next, say a sentence with the word in it (to put the word in the context of a sentence) and then repeat the word. This ensures that the student has heard the word correctly, e.g. "Fainted. The boy fainted when he saw the mouse. Fainted."